"I'm attracted to you."

He was attracted to her? Better yet, he was admitting it? So maybe this thing wasn't one-sided after all.

"And I shouldn't be attracted to you," Egan continued. "It's unprofessional and dangerous. There's a reason for the regulation about a Ranger not getting personally involved with someone in protective custody. A personal involvement could cause me to lose focus. And that could get you killed."

And in that moment, Egan latched on to her wrists, then whirled her around and put her back against the doorframe. He moved closer until his mouth was almost touching hers.

"You don't want a piece of me," Egan warned. She reminded herself of what Egan said about losing focus. Oh, yes. This was the ultimate way to do it.

And she'd never wanted anything so badly in her life.

D0048590

DELORES FOSSEN

QUESTIONING *the* HEIRESS

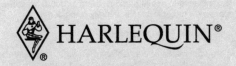

HARLEQUIN®

TORONTO • NEW YORK • LONDON
AMSTERDAM • PARIS • SYDNEY • HAMBURG
STOCKHOLM • ATHENS • TOKYO • MILAN • MADRID
PRAGUE • WARSAW • BUDAPEST • AUCKLAND

To Mallory Kane and Rita Herron.
Thanks so much for this wonderful experience.

ISBN-13: 978-0-373-69342-9
ISBN-10:   0-373-69342-7

QUESTIONING THE HEIRESS

ABOUT THE AUTHOR

Imagine a family tree that includes Texas cowboys, Choctaw and Cherokee Indians, a Louisiana pirate and a Scottish rebel who battled side by side with William Wallace. With ancestors like that, it's easy to understand why Texas author and former Air Force captain Delores Fossen feels as if she was genetically predisposed to writing romances. Along the way to fulfilling her DNA destiny, Delores married an Air Force Top Gun who just happens to be of Viking descent. With all those romantic bases covered, she doesn't have to look too far for inspiration.

Books by Delores Fossen

HARLEQUIN INTRIGUE
913—UNEXPECTED FATHER
932—THE CRADLE FILES
950—COVERT CONCEPTION
971—TRACE EVIDENCE IN TARRANT COUNTY
990—UNDERCOVER DADDY*
1008—STORK ALERT*
1026—THE CHRISTMAS CLUE*
1044—NEWBORN CONSPIRACY*
1050—THE HORSEMAN'S SON*
1075—QUESTIONING THE HEIRESS

*Five-Alarm Babies

Don't miss any of our special offers. Write to us at the following address for information on our newest releases.

Harlequin Reader Service
U.S.: 3010 Walden Ave., P.O. Box 1325, Buffalo, NY 14269
Canadian: P.O. Box 609, Fort Erie, Ont. L2A 5X3

CAST OF CHARACTERS

Sgt. Egan Caldwell—Texas ranger. Dubbed "the surly one" by the wealthy San Antonio residents of Cantara Hills, Egan has one mission—to do his job and prevent anyone else from being murdered in the exclusive community. However, Egan hadn't counted on falling for the killer's next target.

Caroline Stallings—Businesswoman and member of the powerful city board. To stay alive, she joins forces with Egan, but the attraction between them puts Egan in the crosshairs of a killer.

Sgt. Hayes Keller—A Texas Ranger whose own secrets could affect the case.

Lt. Brody McQuade—Head of the Rangers' Unsolved Crimes Unit and in charge of the search to find the Cantara Hills killer.

Taylor Landis—Socialite and Caroline's close friend. Does she unknowingly have information about the murders, and is she, too, in danger?

Miles Landis—Taylor's younger, irresponsible half-brother whose gambling debts might give him a motive for murder.

Carlson Woodward—Egan's childhood nemesis. Would Carlson play a deadly murder game just to prove to himself that he can outsmart Egan and the Rangers?

Kenneth Sutton—The chairman of the city board is powerful and ambitious, but how far will he go to keep himself from being a murder suspect?

Tammy Sutton—Kenneth Sutton's wife. She's seemingly the perfect trophy wife for a powerful politician on his way up.

Walt Caldwell—Egan's father, who's also a chauffeur in Cantara Hills.

Chapter One

San Antonio, Texas

Sgt. Egan Caldwell already had four dead bodies on his hands. He sure as hell didn't want a fifth.

"I need a guard in place by the entrance gate. Now!" he ordered into the thumb-size communicator clipped to his collar. And by God, the two rent-a-cops had better be listening and reacting. "Secure the area and await orders. *Do not fire*. Repeat. Do not fire. If this is our killer, he might have a hostage."

And in this case the hostage would be none other than Caroline Stallings, the Cantara Hills socialite who'd made a frantic call to Egan six minutes earlier. He'd been a Texas Ranger for over four years, and that was more than enough time on the job to have learned that six minutes could be five minutes and fifty-nine seconds too late to save someone from a killer.

With his Sig Sauer Blackwater pistol gripped in his right hand, Egan blinked away the sticky summer rain that was spitting at him, and he zigzagged through the mani-cured shrubs and trees that lined the eighth of a mile-long cobblestone driveway. He'd parked on the street so the sound of his car engine wouldn't alert anyone that he was there. He tried not to make too much noise, listening for anything to indicate the killer was inside the two-story Victorian house. Or worse.

Escaping.

Egan couldn't let this guy get away again.

Things had sure gone to hell in a handbasket tonight. Less than ten minutes ago, Egan had been eating a jalapeño burger, chili fries and going over forensic reports in his makeshift office at the country club. Less than ten minutes ago, the two-hundred-and-eighty-six residents of Cantara Hills had been safe with a Texas Ranger and two civilian guards they'd hired to stop anyone suspicious from getting into the exclusive community.

And then that phone call had come.

"This is Caroline Stallings," she'd said, her voice more breath than sound. Egan had felt her fear from the other end of the line. "There's an intruder in my home."

Then, nothing.

Everything had gone dead.

Well, everything except Egan's concerns. They were sky-high because two of the three previous murders in Cantara Hills and an attempted murder had been preceded by break-ins.

Just like this one.

And even though the person responsible, Vincent Montoya, had been murdered as well, there was obviously someone else. Montoya's boss, maybe. Or someone with a different agenda. Maybe that *someone* was now right there in Caroline Stallings's house.

Egan slapped aside some soggy weeping willow branches

and raced toward the back of the house. He didn't stop. Running, he checked the windows for any sign of the killer or Caroline Stallings. Enough lights were on to illuminate the place, but no one was in sight in the large solarium that he passed.

"I'm at the entry gate," one of the guards said through the communicator. "My partner's by the west fence. That covers both of the most likely exit routes, and San Antonio PD backup should be here soon to cover the others."

Soon wasn't soon enough. He needed backup now.

"I'm going in the house," he told the guard. Egan had to make sure Caroline Stallings was alive and that she stayed that way. "If the intruder comes running out of there *alone,* try to make an arrest. If he doesn't cooperate, if you have to shoot, then aim low for the knees. I want this SOB alive."

Because this particular SOB might be able to answer some hard questions about the four deaths that'd happened in or around Cantara Hills in the past nine months.

Egan glanced around to make sure the intruder hadn't escaped into the back or east yards. If he had, then it was a long drop down since the house was literally perched on the lip of a jagged limestone bluff. An escape over that particular wrought-iron fence could be suicide. But Egan did spot someone.

The brunette with a butcher knife.

She was standing just a few feet away on the porch near double stained-glass doors, and she had a white-knuckled grip on the gleaming ten-inch blade. Her blue-green eyes were wide, her chest pumping with jolts of breath that strained her sleeveless turquoise top.

It was Caroline Stallings.

Alive, thank God. And she seemed unharmed.

Egan had seen her around Cantara Hills a couple of times in the past week since the Texas Rangers had been called in to solve three cold-case murders and then a hot one that'd happened only forty-eight hours earlier. During those other sightings, Ms. Stallings had always appeared so cool, rich and collected. She wasn't so cool or collected now with her shaky composure and windswept dark brown hair.

But the rich part still applied.

Despite the fear and that god-awful big knife, she looked high priced, high rent and high maintenance.

She jumped when she saw him. And gasped. That caused her chest to pump even harder.

"Where's the intruder?" Egan mouthed.

She used the knife blade to point in the direction of the left side of the house. The opposite location from where he'd come. "My bedroom," she mouthed back. "I ran out here when I heard the noise."

Wise move. From her vantage point, she could see a lot through that beveled glass, including an intruder if he was about to come after her.

She reached over, eased open the door, and Egan slipped inside through the kitchen. The floor was gray slate. Potentially noisy. So he lightened his steps.

There were yards of slick black granite countertops, stainless appliances that reflected like mirrors, and in the open front cabinets, precise rows of crystal glasses, all shimmering and cool. He lifted an eyebrow at the half-empty bag of Oreo cookies on the kitchen island.

The A/C spilled over him, chilling the rain that snaked down his face and back. "Has the intruder come out of your bedroom or moved past you to get to another part of the house?" he asked.

"No one's come out of that room," she insisted.

So Egan turned his ear in that direction and listened.

Well, that's what he tried to do, anyway, but he couldn't hear much, other than Caroline Stallings's frantic breathing and her silk clothes rustling against her skin. She was obviously trembling from head to toe.

"When I came home from work, I noticed my security system wasn't working. Then I heard someone moving around in my bedroom," she muttered. "I dialed 9-1-1, they dispatched my call to you, and something or someone cut the line."

Yes. The line had indeed gone dead. Egan had hoped it was because of the rain, but his gut told him otherwise. It wasn't difficult to cut a phone line or disarm a security system, and perps usually did that when they wanted to sever their victim's means of communication. Murder or something equally nasty usually followed. Hopefully, he'd prevented the "equally nasty" part from happening.

"And I found this thing in my car," she added a moment later.

The vague *thing* got his attention. That wasn't good, either. Egan didn't want his attention on anything other than the intruder.

He glanced over his shoulder at Ms. Stallings and scowled at her so she'd hush. The scowl was still on his face when he heard the sound. Not breathing or rustlings on silk. It came from the direction of her bedroom, and it sounded as if someone had opened a door.

"What's the status of SAPD?" Egan whispered into the communicator.

"Not here yet," was the guard's response.

Egan silently cursed. It was decision time. He could stand there and continue to protect Ms. Stallings, or he could do something to catch a possible killer.

It didn't take him but a second to decide.

"Follow me," he instructed Caroline. "Stay low and don't make a sound."

She nodded and kept a firm grip on the butcher knife.

"And don't accidentally stab me with that thing," he snarled.

She tossed him a scowl of her own.

Egan took his first steps toward the bedroom, moving from the slate floor of the kitchen to some kind of exotic hardwood in the dining room and the foyer. He stopped. Listened. But he didn't hear any indication that the intruder was coming their way. So he took another step. Then, another. Caroline Stallings followed right behind him.

From the massive foyer, it was well over twenty feet to her bedroom. The door was open, and he paused in the entryway to get a look around. It, too, was massive. At least four hundred square feet. He wasn't surprised by all the space.

There were more dark hardwood floors and an equally dark four-poster bed frame, but nearly everything else was virginal white. The walls, the rugs, the high-end dresser and chest that were glossy white wood. It smelled like linen, starch and the rain.

No visible intruder.

However, there was movement.

Egan spun in that direction, re-aiming his weapon, but he realized the movement had come from the gauzy white curtains that were stirring in the breeze. He quickly spotted the breeze's source. Another set of French doors.

And these were wide open.

The doors shifted a little with each new brush of wind. That was obviously the sound he'd heard when he'd thought the intruder was escaping.

Mentally cursing again, Egan stepped just inside the room so he could get a better look at the floor. It didn't take any Ranger training or skill to see the wet footprints on the hardwood. The prints didn't just lead into the room. There were also some going out.

Hell. The intruder had likely left before Egan had even arrived.

"The cops are here," the guard informed Egan through the communicator.

Maybe it wasn't too late. "Have them check the grounds, but it looks as if our guy got away."

"He got away?" Caroline repeated with more than a bit of anger in her voice.

She went forward until she was right at his back and came up on her tiptoes so she could peer over his shoulder. She touched him in the process. Specifically, her silk-covered right breast swished against his back. That didn't stop her from looking and obviously seeing those tracks.

"He's gone," she mumbled, moving back slightly. She cursed, too, and it wasn't exactly mild. But it was justified. Judging from what the Rangers had learned about the murders, Caroline Stallings just might be on the killer's list.

The problem was—who was the killer?

And why exactly would he want Caroline dead?

So far, all the victims had been connected to a fatal hit-and-run that'd happened nine months earlier on the night of a high-society Christmas party at Cantara Hills. The now-dead Vincent Montoya was responsible for that incident, in which a young woman had died. In fact, everyone directly connected to the hit-and-run was dead.

Except for Caroline.

She'd been driving the vintage sports car that Vincent Montoya had slammed into.

Caroline had been injured, too, and supposedly lost her memory of not only the accident but that entire fateful night. The so-called amnesia bothered the hell out of Egan. Was she faking it to save one of her rich friends who might have caused the hit-and-run? Or was she covering for herself because she'd been negligent in some way? Egan didn't know which, but he was almost positive she was covering something.

Almost.

"The police will come inside any minute," Egan told her. He moved her back into the doorway so that she'd be away from the windows. "Then, I can question you and have them check for trace and prints. We might be able to get something off those shoe impressions and the doorknobs."

He didn't want to get too engrossed in processing the crime scene just in case the cops flushed out the intruder and the SOB came running back into the house. That's the reason Egan kept his service pistol aimed and ready.

"You're sure you had your security system turned on?" he asked her.

"Of course. Since the murders, I always make sure it's set. But as I said, it wasn't working when I came home." She looked around. "At least nothing appears to have been ransacked. And besides, there wasn't much to steal since I don't keep money or expensive jewelry in the house."

"This person might not have been after stuff," Egan grumbled.

She touched the highly polished dresser, which was dotted with perfectly aligned silver-framed photos of what appeared to be family members. "Do you think the intruder could have been the person who murdered Vincent Montoya?"

"It's possible." More than possible. Likely. Especially since the ritzy neighborhood of Cantara Hills had been virtually crime-free prior to the hit-and-run. But afterward… Well, that was a whole different story.

"Why isn't Lt. McQuade here?" she asked a moment later. "I figured he'd be the one to come."

Brody McQuade, the Ranger lieutenant in charge of the Cantara Hills murders. "He's in California trying to track down a person of interest."

"Oh. Then what about the other Ranger—Sgt. Keller?" She spoke in a regular voice. Not whispers. And Egan didn't have to listen hard to that shiny accent to know that she didn't seem to care for his presence. "He was at the country club earlier. Why didn't he come?"

"Hayes is in Austin at the crime lab. And before you ask, I'm in charge of this investigation right now, and you're stuck with me."

"Stuck with the surly one," she mumbled. Her chin came up when he glared back at her. "That's what people around here call you. Brody's the intense one. Hayes is the chip-on-the-shoulder one."

Egan's glare morphed into a frown. "And I got named 'the surly one'? That's the best you people could do?"

She nodded as if his *you-people* insult didn't bother her in the least. "It suits you."

Yeah. It did. But for some reason it riled him, coming from her. "You're the *richer* one."

"Excuse me?" She blinked.

Egan tried not to smile at her obvious indignation. "There are three young Cantara Hills socialites involved in this investigation. The 'rich' one is your lawyer friend, Victoria Kirkland. You're the 'richer' one. And Taylor Landis, the third socialite, who hosted that infamous Christmas party, is the 'richest of them all.'"

She gave him a flat look. "How original. That must have required lots of time and mental energy to come up with those."

"About as much time and energy as it took you and your pals to come up with *surly.*"

They stared at each other.

There was a sharp rap at the front door, causing both Egan and her to jump a little. But even a little jump for Egan was an embarrassing annoyance and more proof that Caroline Stallings was a distraction he didn't need or want.

"SAPD," the man said from outside the door. "We can't find anyone on the grounds."

Egan didn't even bother with profanity—he was past that point. He went to the door and let the two uniformed officers in. Both were drenched from the rain, as were the two security guards behind them. That same drenching rain would likely wash away any tracks or evidence that the intruder had left in the yard.

"There are shoe prints in the bedroom," Egan informed them, and he hitched his thumb in that direction. "It looks as if that's the point of entry and escape. I want that entire area processed."

The taller Hispanic cop nodded. "I'll get our CSI guys

out here right away." He paused and looked at Caroline. "What about her? Does she need medical attention?"

"I'm fine," she insisted.

Egan slipped his pistol back into his leather shoulder holster. "Secure the crime scene," he instructed the officer. "Check for signs of forcible entry and a cut phone line. Someone probably tampered with the security system, too. And let me know the minute the CSI guys arrive. Ms. Stallings has to show me a *thing* she found in her car, and I'll question her about the intruder while I'm doing that."

"Oh, yes. *The thing,*" Caroline said as if she'd forgotten all about it. "My car's in the garage. This way." She led him through the foyer and back into the kitchen—all thirty to forty feet of it. She slid the knife back into the empty slot of a granite butcher's block.

"You're sure you didn't see this person in your house?" Egan proceeded.

"No. Not even a shadow."

Egan kept at it. "But you heard a sound. Footsteps, maybe?"

"I'm not sure what I heard. Movement, yes. But not footsteps per se."

Too bad. The sound of footsteps could have given him possible information about the size of the intruder. Since they were nearing the solarium and the garage, Egan shifted his focus a little. "What exactly is this thing you found in your car?"

"A little black plastic box about the size of a man's wallet. It fell out from beneath my dash while I was driving home tonight."

That didn't immediately alarm him. "And you don't

think it's part of the car?" Though he couldn't imagine what part of the car that would be, exactly.

She lifted her shoulder. "I guess it could be. But it'd been secured with duct tape."

Now, the alarms came. She wasn't the sort of woman to buy anything that required the use of duct tape. "Did you open this box?"

"No. It fell as I was pulling into my garage so I let it stay put and went inside. I'd left my cell phone at the restaurant in the country club, and I was going to use my house phone to call someone about the box, but then I heard the intruder."

So, she'd had two surprises in one night. Were they connected? "What do you think this box could be?"

"Maybe some kind of eavesdropping equipment," she readily supplied. "My family and I are in the antiques business. Competition is a lot more aggressive than you'd think, and I'm within days of closing a multimillion-dollar deal."

That silenced some of those alarms in Egan's head. "So you think your competition could have planted a listening device to get insider information?"

"It's possible."

Egan followed her through the massive solarium. More lights flared on as they walked through, and those lights gave him a too-good view of his hostess's backside. In that short black skirt, it was hard not to notice that particular part of her anatomy. Ditto for her long legs, which looked even longer because of the three-inch heels she was wearing. She was no waif, that was for sure. Caroline Stallings had a woman's body with plenty of curves.

"The garage is through here," she explained, and she reached for a door.

Egan caught on to her arm and pulled her behind him.

There was renewed alarm in her eyes. "You think the intruder could still be around?"

"No. But I don't want you to take any unnecessary chances. I want you alive and well because if you ever get your memory back, we might finally be able to figure out who's behind these killings."

She made a noncommittal sound. "And that's why you set up the appointment for the day after tomorrow for me to see the psychiatrist. The one who specializes in recovering lost memories from traumatic incidents. She wants to try some new drug on me."

Egan didn't think it was his imagination that Caroline was upset about that. Probably because it threw off her daily massage schedule or something. But he didn't care one bit about inconveniencing her. He only wanted the truth about what'd really happened the night of that hit-and-run.

"The psychiatrist also wants me to keep a journal of my dreams," she added. "I was up at three in the morning writing down things that I'm sure won't make a bit of sense to her. I just don't think this'll do any good."

"You never know," he mumbled. "It might be the key to the truth." But even a long shot like this was a move in the right direction.

He preceded her into the garage. The lights were still on, and there were two cars parked inside. A vintage white Mercedes convertible, top up, beaded with rainwater, and a 1966 candy-apple-red Mustang with a coat of dust on it. What Egan didn't see were any signs of the person who'd left those tracks in her bedroom.

"The box thing is in the Mercedes," she volunteered, stepping ahead of Egan. She, too, made vigilant glances all around them. But the vigilance didn't seem necessary because no one jumped out at them, and no one was lurking between the vehicles.

She opened the passenger's door and pointed to the object on the floor. *Yep*. It was a small black box all right, and it had strips of black duct tape dangling off the sides.

"Like I said, I think it's an eavesdropping device," she commented.

And she reached for it.

Her fingers were less than an inch away when Egan practically tackled her so he could snag her wrist. In theory, it was a good idea because he didn't want her to smear any prints that might be on the box. But that snagged wrist and his forward momentum sent them sprawling onto the passenger's seat.

Caroline landed face-first. He landed with his face in her peach-scented, shoulder-length hair. And another part of him, a brainless part of him, hit against her firm butt. Egan grunted from the contact.

Her body nearly distracted him from hearing the tiny, soft sounds.

Clicks.

But Egan shook his head, mentally amending that. Not clicks.

Ticks.

The sounds were synchronized. One right behind the other. Marking off time.

Or rather counting it down.

Hell.

"Get out of here!" he shouted, dragging Caroline from the seat. "It's a bomb."

Chapter Two

Before Egan Caldwell's words even registered in Caroline's head, he already had hold of her and was running toward the door with her in tow.

Mercy, was that black box really a bomb?

She'd heard the ticking sound, of course. Not while she'd been in the car earlier when the engine was running. But now—when Egan and she had tumbled onto the seat. She seriously doubted that an eavesdropping device would have a timer on it.

The adrenaline jolted through her, and Caroline somehow managed to run in her unsensible business heels. Probably thanks to Egan. He had a death grip on her left wrist and practically plowed them through the door that led to a narrow mudroom and then the solarium on the back of her house.

"Evacuate now—there's a bomb in the garage!" he shouted. Which, in turn, caused more shouts from the cops and the security guards.

All of them began to run. Egan didn't stop, either. He hauled her through the kitchen, then the living room, and they exited through the front door, on the opposite side of the house from the garage. The cops were ahead of them. The two civilian guards, behind.

The rain was coming down harder now and lashed at them like razors. So did the blinding blue strobe lights from the police cruiser parked at the end of her cobblestone drive. It didn't hinder Egan. He barreled down the front porch steps with her and made a beeline to the driveway, getting her even farther away from the garage.

"Call the bomb squad," Egan shouted over his shoulder to one of the guards who was sprinting along behind them. He glanced around through the rain and the night until his attention landed on the other guard. "Keep everyone away from the house."

Because the place might blow up.

That "bottom line" realization sent Caroline's heart to her knees. Someone might get hurt. Also, her house might soon be destroyed, and there was apparently nothing she could do to stop it.

But who had done this?

A car bomb certainly seemed like overkill for an overly zealous competitor in the antiques business. *Sweet heaven.* Had the intruder also been the one to plant that bomb? And if so, why?

Of course, she couldn't discount the four previous murders. All people she'd known. All of them involved in some way with the City Board, of which she was a member.

Was she now the killer's next target?

Her legs and thighs began to cramp from the exertion. She wasn't much of a runner, and the heels didn't help. Caroline was wheezing for breath and her heart was hammering in her chest by the time they made it to the end of her drive.

Egan stopped, finally, and pulled her in front of him. Actually, he put her against the wet stone pylon that held the open wrought-iron gate in place. He got right behind her, pushing her face-first against the stones.

"Don't look back," he warned. "And shelter your eyes just in case that damn thing goes off."

That's when she realized he was *sheltering* her. It wasn't personal; Caroline was sure of that. She'd seen the disdain in his eyes. Sgt. Egan Caldwell was merely doing his job, and right now, she was the job.

"You really think the bomb's about to explode?" Caroline asked.

"It's a possibility, but I don't believe the device is large enough to create a blast that'll reach us here. At least, I hope not," he added in a mumble.

But the officers apparently didn't believe that because one of them began to sprint in the direction of her nearest neighbor. "I'll have them evacuate," the Hispanic cop relayed to Egan.

Mercy. Now her neighbor and best friend, Taylor Landis, was perhaps in danger.

Caroline wiped her hand over her face to sling off some of the rainwater. She wished she could do the same to the adrenaline and fear because it was starting to overwhelm her. "This doesn't make sense."

"If we have a vigilante killer on our hands, it doesn't have to make sense," he reminded her.

Yes. She'd heard that theory. Or rather the gossip. That Vincent Montoya might have been murdered by a vigilante who maybe wanted to tie up all loose ends of the hit-and-run.

"I can understand why a vigilante would go after Montoya," she mumbled. "But why try to kill me?"

"You got an answer for that?" Egan asked.

Since that sounded like some kind of challenge, she looked back at him. She didn't have to look far. He was there. Right over her soaking wet shoulder, and the overhead security light clearly showed his rain-streaked face.

Surly, beyond doubt.

Caroline tried not to let the next thought enter her mind, but she couldn't stop it. Egan Caldwell was a good-looking man. Okay, he wasn't just good-looking.

He was hot.

Dark blond hair, partially hidden beneath that creamy-white Stetson. Eyes that were a brilliant, burning blue. He had just enough ruggedness to stop him from being a pretty boy and just enough pretty boy to smooth out some of that ruggedness.

And Caroline hated she'd noticed that about him.

"What are you waiting for me to say?" she snapped. "That this guy wants me dead because I saw or heard something the night of the hit-and-run?" She didn't pause long enough for him to confirm it because Caroline could see the confirmation in those eyes. "Well, if that were true, why didn't he come after me nine months ago? If this is truly some vigilante killer, then I should have been one of the first on his list."

Egan stood there, staring at her, with the summer rain assaulting them and the sounds of chaos going on all around. The cruiser's lights pulsed blue flashes over him. Flashes that were the same color as his eyes. "Maybe the killer hasn't come after you before because you supposedly have no memories of the hit-and-run."

Again, that wasn't new information, either. "Nothing has changed about that. It's not *supposedly*." Caroline froze and then eased around so that she was facing him. "But I have an appointment the day after tomorrow to see that psychiatrist to help me remember what happened."

He nodded and snorted slightly as if annoyed that it'd taken her so long to figure it out. "Did you tell anyone about that appointment?"

Oh, mercy. "Yes. I was talking about it today when I had lunch at the Cantara Hills Country Club." Actually, Caroline had verbally blasted the Rangers, Egan and Brody, for demanding the appointment. She'd already been through hours of therapy and had zero recollection of the time immediately before, during and following the accident. The dream log and the appointment seemed not only unnecessary but intrusive and a total waste of time—and hope.

"Who was there at this country club lunch?" Egan asked. He used his snarly Texas Rangers' tone that was only marginally softened by his easy drawl. Words slid right off that drawl.

"My parents. They were leaving on vacation this afternoon, a second honeymoon they've been planning for months, and I wanted to see them before they left." In the distance, she could hear the sirens. Probably the bomb squad. Maybe they'd get there in time to disarm it before it could hurt anyone. "And Kenneth Sutton and his wife, Tammy, joined us."

His mouth tightened. "Kenneth, who's chairman of the City Board. He's also a suspect."

"Only because the hit-and-run driver, Vincent Montoya, worked for him. But Kenneth told me he had no idea what Montoya had done."

"Yeah, yeah," Egan grumbled. "Because according to Kenneth, Vincent Montoya killed Kimberly McQuade in that crash because he was jealous she'd rebuffed him and had had an affair with another man. An affair she'd never mentioned to anyone. Funny that the guy's never surfaced, either, and there's not a lick of proof that Montoya had had any sexual interest in Kimberly. Or vice versa. According to people who knew her well, Vincent Montoya wasn't her type."

"Because he was a lowly driver?" Caroline instantly regretted her question. It sounded snobby, especially since Egan's own father was a chauffeur. And not just any old chauffeur but the one who worked for her father's close friend who lived in Cantara Hills.

"I'm sorry," she mumbled. "Talking about that night isn't easy for me." Caroline was still grieving. Always would. There wasn't a day that went by that she didn't regret what had happened. Yes, Montoya had caused the fatal crash, but Caroline couldn't help but wonder if there was something she could have done to stop it.

"Murder is rarely easy to talk about," he countered.

When Caroline continued, she softened her voice. "I'm just having a hard time believing that Kenneth Sutton, a man I work with on the City Board, a man I've known my entire life, is capable of ordering his driver to murder someone. Yet the Rangers seem to think that might have happened."

"You might think that, too, once I've had a chance to question Kenneth further and have more information." He shrugged. "But the point right now is Kenneth was there today at lunch with you. He heard you say that you had an appointment with the shrink. Who else heard?"

She started to shake her head but stopped. Oh, this was

not good. "My parents, Kenneth and his wife were the only people at the table with me, but some of my other neighbors were there. They could have heard."

"Give me names," he demanded, while he made a visual check of the area around them.

"Your father's boss, Link Hathaway, and his daughter, Margaret. Miles Landis was there, too. He's my best friend's brother. Half brother," she corrected. Miles had dropped by to hit her up for a loan, again. Caroline had turned him down, again. "Your father even came into the restaurant for a couple of minutes to talk to Link."

Egan mumbled some profanity under his breath. "So, what you're saying is that everyone in Cantara Hills knows about your appointment?"

She silently repeated the same profanity as Egan. "Yes. But I didn't think I had to keep it a secret. My parents and I were discussing it because my mom's upset about me being sedated with this drug and then interrogated. She wanted to cancel her trip, and I had to talk her out of it."

Egan jumped right on that. "Why is she upset?"

Caroline groaned. The adrenaline and bomb scare had obviously made her chatty. "Long story."

"I'm listening."

Of course he was. And he was scowling again. He apparently thought she was concerned about revealing something incriminating.

Which she was.

In a way.

But Caroline couldn't think about that now, and she didn't dare voice any of it to Egan. She'd already blabbed enough tonight.

She chose her words carefully. "My mother's afraid I'll

say something about a personal incident, and that the information will get around to everyone," she admitted. "The incident isn't pertinent to this case."

"I'll be the judge of that."

Caroline was sure her scowl matched his, and she had to speak through nearly clenched teeth. "All right. Three years ago I was involved with a jerk. Everybody knows about the broken engagement, but no one else knows that the jerk stole money from my parents. I want to keep it that way, understand?"

Egan responded with a noncommittal grunt. "I'll keep it that way if I decide it's not vital information that can help me catch a killer. You're not my priority, Ms. Stallings. And neither is your parents' need to keep their skeletons shut away in their walk-in closet."

"Oh, God," she mumbled, ignoring his last zinger. She checked her watch. "My parents. They'll be in Cancun by now, and one of the neighbors might have called them at their hotel. They'll be worried." She glanced in the direction of her parents' house. Just up the street. And even though she knew her parents weren't home, her concerns were verified.

The cruiser's lights had attracted the neighbors. All of them. One of the officers was guarding the street in front of her house and preventing anyone from getting too close. Including her parents' nearest neighbors, the Jenkins. She spotted them, a perky yellow umbrella perched over their heads. They were frantically waving at her, and Mrs. Jenkins had a cell phone pressed to her ear.

"They say they have your parents on the line. They want to know if you're all right," the officer relayed to

her. Because of the sirens and the rain, he had to practically shout.

"Tell them I'm fine," Caroline shouted back. "And that
I love them. I'll call them later."

If Egan had any response to her message, he didn't
show it. He looked at the approaching trio of bomb squad
vehicles before turning his attention back to her. "Other
than you, who had access to your car today?"

It was something that hadn't occurred to Caroline. Yet.
But it would have once she'd caught her breath. "I was
the only person in the car. My family's business office is
on San Pedro Avenue, and I parked there in my space in
the building garage. I came back here to Cantara Hills for
lunch around noon, and then I met with a client at his
office just off Highway 281 before returning to work."

He glanced around them again. "I noticed your car
doors were unlocked in the garage. Were they locked
when you were at any of these other places?"

Caroline really hated to admit this, but, hey, she hadn't
known that her every movement might have been watched
by a killer. "I had the top down most of the day so it
wouldn't have been hard for anyone to get inside. And
since it's a vintage car and I don't keep anything valuable
inside, it doesn't have a security alarm."

The bomb squad vehicles braked to a stop by the gate.

Egan stared at her. "So anyone could have overheard
your conversation at lunch, and those same anyones could
have gained access to your car and planted a bomb."

Because he made her sound like a careless idiot,
Caroline frowned. "That about sums it up."

But Egan was right. She hadn't been cautious, driving
with the car top down with a killer on the loose, and it

could have cost others their lives. She already blamed herself for Kimberly McQuade's death.

She didn't want this on her conscience as well.

The bomb squad personnel barreled out of their vehicles, and Egan stepped away from her to speak to a burly blond man wearing dark blue-gray body armor. Caroline listened as Egan briefed the man, describing the location of the device and the size.

The man tipped his head toward her. "Go ahead and get her out of here. I want those guards and uniforms out, too. I don't want anyone near the place until my guys have checked out this thing."

Egan turned back to her. There was more displeasure in his body language and expression, probably because he had to babysit her.

"Let's go," he grumbled.

But the grumble had barely left Egan's mouth when the sound of the blast rocketed behind them.

Chapter Three

Well, at least no one was dead.

That was the only good thing Egan could say about the events of the night.

First, an intruder. The intruder's escape. Then, an explosion. Egan was waiting for a call from the bomb squad so he'd know the extent of the damage, but he didn't have to hear a situation report to confirm that the killer had a new target.

Caroline Stallings.

She was in the corner of his temporary office. Soaked to the bone. She'd gotten even wetter when they had run from his car and into the country club. Her clothes were clinging to her body, and there were drops of rain still sliding down her bare legs and into those pricey, uncomfortable-looking heels. She was shivering. And using his phone to call her parents in Cancun, Mexico. Her calm, practically lively tone didn't go with her slumped shoulders and shell-shocked expression. The rain, and possibly even a tear or two, had streaked through what was left of her makeup.

"No. I'm fine, really," she assured her parents. "There's nothing you can do, and I have everything under control."

She caught her bottom lip between her teeth for a moment, probably to stop it from trembling. "I'm with one of the Rangers," she went on. "We're at his office at the Cantara Hills Country Club." She paused. "No. I'm with Sgt. Egan Caldwell." Another pause. "No." She glanced at him and turned away. "He's the surly one," she whispered.

Egan was just punchy enough that he couldn't stop himself from smiling. He didn't let Caroline see it, of course.

While she continued her call, Egan went to the closet behind his desk and took out one of the four freshly laundered shirts hanging inside. His jeans were soaked, too, but changing them would require leaving Caroline alone. Because they had a killer on the loose, that wasn't a good idea. So he settled for a fresh blue button-up. Either that or a white shirt and jeans were his standard "uniform" when he was on duty, which lately was 24/7. He changed and put back on his shoulder holster. Later, he'd have to give his gun a good cleaning to dry it out as well.

"Please don't come home," he heard Caroline say. She'd repeated a variation of that at least a half-dozen times since the call began. "Yes, I'll have the locks changed on all the doors and windows at the house. I'll make sure the security system is checked. And I won't stay there alone. I promise." She shivered again. "I love you, too."

She'd said that at least a half-dozen times as well. *I love you.* The words were heartfelt. It was hard to fake that level of emotion. Even though he was thirty years old and had been in his share of relationships, it still amazed Egan that some people could say those words so easily.

Not him.

But then, he'd never tried, figuring he was more likely to choke on them than say them aloud.

He finished transferring his badge to the dry shirt, turned, and Caroline was there holding out his phone for him to take. "Thank you," she said. No more fake cheerfulness. The shock was setting in, and she was shaking harder now.

Egan hung up the phone, extracted another of his shirts from the closet and handed it to her. "Put this on. As soon as the bomb squad clears the area, you can go to your friend's house and get some dry clothes." That might not happen soon, though, and her friends wouldn't be able to get to her since no one could use the road to drive to the country club. The bomb squad had sectioned it off.

She made a small throaty sound of agreement and slipped on his shirt. "Thank you again."

Caroline wearily sank down into the studded burgundy leather chair next to his desk and closed her fingers over the delicate gold heart necklace that had settled in her cleavage. Like the words to her parents, she'd done that a lot tonight as well.

Egan anticipated what she'd do next. She was wearing two dainty gemstone gold rings on her left hand. Opals on one. Aquamarines on the other. Another opal ring was on her right hand. She began to twist and adjust them. She was obviously trying to settle her nerves. But Egan was betting that settled nerves weren't in her immediate future no matter how many rings she twisted.

"I suppose the bomb squad will call when they know anything," she said. Not really a question. He'd already explained that.

Still, Egan nodded and started a fresh pot of coffee. Thank God for the little premeasured packets because that was the only chance he had of making it drinkable, and right now, he needed massive quantities of caffeine that he could consume in a hurry so he could stay alert and fight off the inevitable adrenaline crash.

"You didn't get to finish your dinner." Caroline pushed her damp hair from her face and tipped her head to the now-cold burger and fries on the center of his desk. He'd managed only a few bites.

"It's not the first time." And he hoped that wasn't concern for him in her voice.

Wait.

What was he thinking?

It couldn't be concern. He was the surly one, and she was the richer one. She was an heiress. He, the chauffeur's son. Concern on her part wasn't in this particular equation, and the only thing she cared about was getting through this. The only thing he cared about was keeping her alive and catching a killer.

The silence came like the soggy downpour that was occurring simultaneously outside. They weren't comfortable with each other, and they weren't comfortable being in the same confined space. Hopefully, that confinement would end when the bomb squad finished, and he could pawn this "richer" leggy brunette off on someone else.

Anyone else.

"I'm sorry I wasn't able to help more with the investigation of the hit-and-run," Caroline whispered.

That comment/apology came out of the blue, and Egan certainly hadn't expected it. More ring twisting, yes. Ditto for touching that gold heart pendant. But he hadn't anticipated a sincere-sounding apology. "And you're probably sorry that you were driving the car that night."

"That, too." She nodded. "But my memory loss is only of that night. I remember Kimberly."

So did Egan. Kimberly had grown up on the same street that he had. And her brother, Brody, was now Egan's boss.

"She was a kind, generous woman who worked hard as an intern for the City Board," Caroline continued. "I'm glad her killer is dead."

And yet her killer was also someone whom Caroline had known. Vincent Montoya, who'd rammed his vehicle into the passenger's side of Caroline's vintage sports car. The impact had thrown Kimberly from her seat, and she'd sustained a broken neck. Death had come instantly.

But not for the two other men Montoya had murdered.

Two men, Trent Briggs and Gary Zelke, who Montoya likely believed had seen him ram into Caroline's car, had been killed months later. Montoya had murdered them to eliminate witnesses and probably would have done the same to Victoria Kirkland, a third possible witness, if someone—the vigilante maybe—hadn't killed Montoya first. Since it was possible that Victoria was now in danger from this vigilante, she was out of state in Brody's protective custody.

Unlike Caroline.

She was here at Cantara Hills. Right in the line of fire.

"We still need to find out if Montoya was working alone, or if someone hired him to commit those murders," Egan reminded her. He stood and poured them both some coffee. "And if he was working alone, then who's this new intruder who came into your house tonight?"

She took the mug of coffee from him, gripping it in both of her shaky hands, and she sipped some even though it was steaming hot. "And you think that intruder might be Kenneth Sutton, the chairman of the City Board?" Despite all the other emotions, skepticism oozed from her voice.

Egan shrugged and sank down in his chair. "Stating the obvious here, but Montoya was Kenneth Sutton's driver, personal assistant and jack-of-all trades."

"That doesn't mean Kenneth ordered Montoya to kill anyone. Kenneth's a career politician and is running for the governor's office. He can be ambitious when it comes to politics, but I don't think he has murder on his mind."

Egan was about to remind her that rich politicians hid behind their facades just like everybody else, but his cell phone rang, and he snatched it up. "Sgt. Caldwell."

"This is Detective Mark Willows from the bomb squad. We've done a preliminary assessment. No injuries. Property damage is minimal. Definitely nothing structural. A few holes and dents in the garage wall. For the most part, the impact was confined to the Mercedes."

Well, that was better news than he'd expected. That blast had been damn loud. "There was enough damage to destroy the car?" Egan asked.

"It's banged up pretty bad, but we'll tow it to the crime lab and look for prints and other evidence. The explosion happened at 8:10 p.m. You'll probably want to question the owner to see if there's anything significant about that time. We'll question her, too, but it can wait until tomorrow. We'll be here most of the night collecting the bits and pieces so we can reassemble the device and try to figure out who made it."

"Thanks. Call me if you have anything else." Egan

clicked the end-call button and looked at Caroline. Who was looking at him, obviously waiting. "Good news," he let her know. "No one was hurt. Your car is totaled, but the house is okay."

The breath swooshed out of her, and her hand was suddenly shaking so hard that she sloshed some coffee on her fingers when she set the cup on his desk.

"Good. That's good." A moment later, she repeated it.

He debated if he should check her fingers, to make sure she hadn't scalded them. She certainly wasn't doing anything about it. Egan finally reached over and caught on to her wrist so he could have a look. Yep. Definitely red fingers. He rolled his chair across the floor to get to the small fridge, retrieved a cold can of soda and rolled back toward her. He pressed the can to her fingers.

She didn't resist. Caroline just sat there. Her head hung low. Probably numb. Maybe even in shock. "I didn't want anyone else's death or injuries on my hands," she said under her breath. "I couldn't live with that."

Since she seemed on the verge of tears, or even a total meltdown, Egan decided to get her mind back on business. His mind, too. He didn't like seeing her like this.

Vulnerable.

Fragile.

Tormented.

He preferred when she had that aristocratic chin lifted high and the ritzy sass was in her eyes. Because there was no way he could ever be interested in someone with a snobby, rich, stubborn chin. But the vulnerability and the genuine ache he heard in her whisper, that could draw him in.

Oh, yeah.

It could make him see her as an imperfect, desirable woman and not the next victim on a killer's list.

And that wouldn't be good for either Caroline or him. He needed to focus.

That was the best way to keep her alive and catch a killer.

He wrapped her fingers around the soda and leaned back to put some distance between them. No more touching. No more thinking about personal stuff. "The timer on the explosive was set for 8:10 p.m. Where would you normally have been at that time?"

Her head came up, and she met his gaze. "Since it's Monday, I should have been in the car, driving home from work."

He was afraid she was going to say that. "That's your usual routine?"

She nodded. "I always work late on Mondays. The security guard walks me out to my car at eight p.m., because that's when his shift is over. I leave at exactly that time so he won't have to stay any longer, and it takes me about fifteen minutes to drive home." She put the soft drink can aside so she could touch the necklace. "But the security guard wasn't feeling well tonight. He wouldn't go home until I did so I left about forty-five minutes earlier than I usually do."

That insistent sick guard had saved her life. Egan didn't need to spell that out for her.

"Who knows your work routine?" he asked.

The color drained from her cheeks. "Anyone who knows me."

Well, that didn't narrow it down much, and it certainly didn't exclude Kenneth Sutton. There was just something about Kenneth that reminded Egan of a snake oil salesman. Egan only hoped that his feelings weren't skewed that way because the guy was stinkin' rich.

"So did the same person plant that bomb and then break into my house?" Caroline asked.

"Possibly. Maybe he set the explosive to make sure you didn't come home when he was there."

She shook her head. "Why? If that explosive had killed me, why bother to break into my house?" She waited a moment, her gaze still connected with Egan's. "Unless he was there to make sure I hadn't survived."

It was Egan's turn to shake his head. Egan had already played around with that theory, and it had a major flaw. "Then the intruder would have been lying in wait and would have attacked the moment you walked in. You wouldn't have had time to make that 9-1-1 call or grab a knife."

She closed her eyes a moment, and her breath shuddered. "So, this intruder perhaps not only wanted me dead but also wanted something from my house?"

"Bingo." That was the conclusion he'd reached as well. "He probably thought you'd died in the car bomb, but when you came driving up, he'd perhaps already gotten what he came for or, rather, had tried to do that, and he fled because a person who sets a delayed explosive isn't someone who wants a face-to-face meeting with their victim. Now, the question is—what did he take? The usual is either money or jewelry. Something lightweight enough to carry away."

"I already told you I don't keep large sums of money in the house, or on me. I use plastic for almost everything I buy. And I don't own a lot of jewelry." Caroline held up her hands. "These pieces are all from family members. Aunts and my mother. My grandmother," she added, pointing to the gold heart necklace.

Family stuff. Something else he knew little about. "What about any small valuable antique that the intruder could have taken from your house?"

Another head shake. "I run an antiques business and love vintage cars, but I prefer modern decor." She paused. "Or rather, no decor. I'm not much for fuss or clutter."

He thought of her virginal white bedroom and glistening black kitchen and agreed. Modern, uncluttered and maybe even a little anal. Everything perfectly aligned and in its place, like the cool crystal.

Everything in place but those cookies.

Store-bought. Not the gourmet kind from some chichi bakery. Normal ones. Egan had a hard time imagining her standing in her kitchen. Surrounded by all that expensive glitter. Wearing silk designer clothes. And eating Oreos.

"Wait. There *is* something," she said a moment later. "I have a small clock that was a Christmas gift from my mother. It's portable and probably worth a lot. It's on the nightstand, next to the dream journal I've been keeping for the psychiatrist."

Egan didn't remember seeing a clock or a journal, but then his attention had been on those open French doors, not the nightstand. He grabbed his phone and punched in the number to the SAPD dispatch, who in turn connected him with Detective Mark Willows.

"This is Sgt. Caldwell," he said when Willows answered.

"Glad you called," Willows interrupted before Egan could explain. "I just got an update from the CSI guys. They took Ms. Stallings's lock from her bedroom door so they can test it to see if it was picked. They'll replace it with a temp so we can secure the house."

"Thanks. I'm sure she'll appreciate that."

"Well, we don't want another break-in. This is just preliminary, but those shoe prints left on her bedroom floor are about a size eleven. Some kind of athletic shoes. So, we're probably looking for a male."

Egan made a note to check Kenneth Sutton's shoe size. "I need you to check on the nightstand in the master bedroom and tell me what's there," Egan said to the detective.

"Give me a minute. I'm walking that way." Egan heard the sound of the man's movement. And waited. "There's a phone and a clock," Willows reported. "The phone is white, and the clock is about the size of baseball. It's gold, and it's got pearls and what looks like emeralds all around the dial. Heck, the friggin' hands look like they're made of diamonds. Caldwell, this is some clock."

Yes, and the intruder didn't take it. "Is there anything else on the nightstand?"

"Just a pen. Common, ordinary variety."

Oh, man. "There's no paper or notepad?"

"Nada."

"Thanks. Make sure CSI checks that nightstand for prints." Egan hung up, ready to relay that to Caroline, but he could tell from her expression that she already knew.

"My dream journal is missing," she mumbled.

"Yeah. The expensive clock is still there, though. So, let me guess—everyone at that lunch today heard that you'd been keeping a journal."

The color crept back into her face, and she looked as if she wanted to curse. She nodded.

Hell.

Egan leaned in and looked straight into her eyes. "Caroline, what exactly did you write in that journal?"

Chapter Four

"It's gibberish," Caroline concluded as she glanced over the notes that she'd spent most of the previous night and that morning making. Or, rather, the notes that Egan had *insisted* she make so she could try to re-create her stolen dream journal.

She'd told him the night before that it was futile, that the dreams hadn't revealed anything important. Caroline still believed that. But Egan had persisted anyway, right before the bomb squad had given her the all-clear to leave his office and go to the house of her best friend, Taylor Landis.

Taylor had welcomed Caroline with open arms. Literally. And her friend had hardly let her out of her sight since. They'd chatted, drunk some wine, and then Taylor had called her security expert to go over to Caroline's house to change all the locks on the windows and doors and to repair the security system. It wouldn't give Caroline peace of mind exactly, but it was a start.

"Okay, let me have a look at those notes," Taylor insisted. She had her long blond hair gathered into a ponytail, she gave it an adjustment and then waggled her fingers. "Maybe they won't be gibberish to me."

Caroline handed her the notes and proceeded with her so-called walk-through of her own house. Yet something else Egan had insisted that she do. With an armed security guard shadowing hers and Taylor's every move, Caroline checked her office to make sure everything was in place.

It was.

A PC, laptop and several thousand dollars worth of computer accessories. All still there.

She checked off another room from her list and went to the guest suite off the main corridor. She'd decorated this one all in blue. Pale, barely there blue, for the most part, with the exception of the glossy navy paint on the floor and a fiery abstract oil painting that hung over the natural white stone mantel. She no longer liked that particular bold shade of blue in the painting because it instantly reminded her of Egan's eyes.

Caroline made a mental note to replace it.

"You dreamed about clocks chasing you?" Taylor commented, reading from the reconstructed journal.

"Yes." Caroline frowned. "And don't you dare say anything about ticking biological clocks. I get enough of that from my parents."

"Wouldn't dream of it." However, Taylor's pun indicated she'd thought it. Caroline's frown deepened at her friend's grin.

Caroline checked the white marble guest bathroom. Nothing missing there. And she went into a storage room crammed with carefully stacked, unopened cardboard boxes. Things she'd bought to redecorate when she'd moved from her condo to the house five months earlier. The house had been a thirtieth birthday gift from her parents, and even though she had plenty of space—fourteen rooms—Caroline just hadn't gotten around to making the place *hers*.

She glanced inside the storage room, saw nothing undisturbed and then headed to the one area that she did indeed want to check out.

Her garage.

With her attention nailed to the notes, Taylor followed her. So did the guard, but he kept some distance from them.

"In the dream you had, a man saved you from the attacking clocks," Taylor concluded. "Looks like your rescuer was Egan Caldwell."

Caroline stopped so abruptly that Taylor nearly plowed right into her. "How did you come up with that?"

"Easily. In your notes, you said you were running through the woods with the clocks in pursuit. A man stepped out. He had blond hair, a blue shirt and a silver star embedded in his hand. He shot arrows at the clocks to stop them. Sounds like Egan to me. He has a star badge. He often wears a blue shirt, and he has blondish hair. And if you ask me, those arrows are phallic symbols."

Stunned, Caroline snatched the notes and read over them again. Oh, God. She was certain she hadn't dreamed about Egan and his phallic symbol, but if Taylor believed she had, then Egan might think that as well. She'd have to change the notes before he arrived. Except that she couldn't.

Could she?

No. If he found out, he'd view that as the equivalent of tampering with evidence.

A better solution was just to keep the journal from him and not let him read a single word. She'd wait and show the notes to the psychiatrist, especially since she was meeting with the doctor the following day. Maybe she could convince the psychiatrist to keep them private. After all, it was obvious to her that the dream wasn't connected to the murders or the hit-and-run.

Caroline tucked her journal beneath her arm and stepped into the garage. The doors were open, allowing in the humid breeze and plenty of light so she could see the damage. It was indeed minimal. A few small holes in the wall and some smoke stains—that was it.

Unfortunately, the minimal damage didn't extend to her.

Someone had violated her space, and Caroline wondered how long it would be before she could walk into her house and not think about being killed.

Maybe she never would.

The white Mercedes was gone, of course, towed away in the early hours of the morning by the CSI agents, who were probably now looking for clues about the person who had left that explosive for her. She prayed they'd have answers soon.

Caroline continued to look around the garage, and her gaze landed on the workshop door. It was wide open. And it shouldn't have been. Good grief. She hurried to close it. Except it wouldn't shut. The CSI had apparently busted the lock, probably to check for evidence, and she glanced inside the workshop at what they'd no doubt seen.

Her old secret.

Something she didn't exactly want to announce to the world, including Taylor, who likely knew about it but was too much of a friend to say anything. Caroline would have to do something about getting that door fixed.

Taylor ran her fingers over the remaining vehicle, the 1967 candy-apple-red Mustang. "You used to drive this car all the time," she reminded Caroline.

"Yes. But I gave up on hot, fast things." And for reasons she didn't want to explore, she immediately thought of Egan again.

Thankfully, she didn't have to think of him for long because she heard the voices in her backyard. Obviously, the guard heard them as well because he reached for his gun. Caroline waved him off, however, when she saw her visitors approach the garage.

Kenneth and Tammy Sutton.

She didn't want a gun drawn on her neighbors. Of course, Kenneth was also Egan's prime suspect, but Caroline didn't believe that. Except she hated the uncomfortable feeling that crept through her now. Egan was responsible for those doubts.

But the question was—were his doubts founded?

Twelve hours ago, Caroline would have replied with an emphatic no, but that was before someone had tried to blow her to smithereens.

"Are you all right?" Tammy asked, hurrying to her. She latched on to Caroline, hugging her, and engulfing her in a cloud of Chanel number-something. The woman's layers of thick gold chains dug into Caroline's breasts and her bloodred acrylic nails were like little daggers.

Caroline untangled herself from the hug and stepped back. "I'm fine," she said, realizing she'd been repeating that lie all night and all morning. To her parents. To Taylor. Even to the security guard lurking in the mudroom doorway. And now to Tammy Sutton.

Kenneth strolled closer. No hug. He had his hands in the pockets of his expertly tailored gray suit. With his dark hair combed to perfection, he looked ready for work. And probably was. Being chairman of the City Board often required a sixty-hour-plus week, and it was already past the normal start of his workday.

"You look tired," Kenneth observed.

"Caroline and I sat up chatting all night," Taylor volunteered. Covering for her. So that she wouldn't have to discuss the stress of the explosion and lack of sleep. "She's doing great, just like Caroline always does. Of course, she's anxious to catch the monster who did this."

Kenneth and Tammy nodded sympathetically. "So did the intruder take anything?" Kenneth asked.

Caroline inadvertently glanced down at the new dream journal squished between her arm and side. "Not really."

Tammy must have noticed that glance and the uncertainty in Caroline's voice. "Are you taking inventory?"

"Something like that."

Tammy opened her mouth, probably to ask more, but Caroline heard the movement just a split-second before Egan rounded the corner. Wearing a blue shirt again. And those butt-hugging jeans. No Stetson today. It was probably still drying out from the rain. But he did have his badge and that shoulder holster with the gun tucked inside.

He took one look at Kenneth, and Egan put on his best surly scowl. "Is there a problem?" Egan wanted to know.

"No," Kenneth answered just as quickly. "My wife and I were checking on Caroline. Last I heard, there was no law against that."

Egan's expression didn't change. He went closer to Kenneth and met the man's gaze head-on. "But there are laws against attempted murder, breaking and entering and interfering with an investigation. This is still a crime scene, and you shouldn't be here."

Tammy indignantly pressed her hand to her chest.

"And you don't think we know that this is a crime scene? We're not idiots, Ranger…whatever-your-name-is."

"Caldwell. Remember it, Mrs. Sutton, because you'll see me a lot in the next few days while I interrogate your husband and you." Egan looked down at Kenneth's feet. "What size shoes do you wear?"

"Why?" But it was Tammy who asked, not Kenneth.

"Because I want to know." His attention landed on her shoes as well. "And while you're at it, you can tell me your size, too."

"A perfect six," Tammy said, overly enunciating the words. "And my husband wears a size ten. Satisfied?"

"Not really. I'll have one of the CSI guys drop by to check your closet, just to make sure everything is as *perfect* as you say."

Taylor cleared her throat, obviously sensing that something even more impolite was about to be said, and she went to Kenneth and Tammy. She hooked her arms around both their waists. "Why don't you come on over to my house for some coffee? Egan and Caroline have to finish up this investigation, and we'd just be in the way."

Tammy looked back at Caroline. "Are you sure you don't need us here? Your mother will never forgive me if I don't try to help you at a time like this."

"I'm okay." Caroline hoped. "Please tell Mom that if you talk to her."

Egan looked at the security guard once Kenneth, Tammy and Taylor were out of sight. "Make sure Kenneth Sutton and his wife leave the premises. I don't want them back here, either."

The guard nodded and went after them.

"Tammy's a suspect now?" Caroline asked.

Egan shrugged. "Just about everyone around here is. Guilt by association."

Caroline had the eerie feeling that he wasn't exaggerating. "And her motive?"

"Well, if her husband did order Vincent Montoya to kill those people, then maybe Tammy wants to keep that their own little family secret. Of course, Kenneth has the same motive, so I'd prefer neither of them comes around here."

She huffed. "They're my neighbors. And Kenneth is my boss at the City Board. Any suggestions how to stop them from visiting?"

His gaze eased to hers. "I think my presence will deter them." She stared at him, but he didn't say more. Instead, he shifted his focus to the Mustang. "Nice car."

Yes. It was. "It's from my wild-child days. I guess I'll have to use it for transportation until I can replace the Mercedes." Of course, she was using the Mercedes because her other vehicle had been totaled in the hit-and-run.

His eyebrow lifted. "You were a wild child?" he said in the same tone as if he'd asked if she were a convicted felon.

"Afraid so. Six speeding tickets my senior year in college."

That earned her a hmmph. "Speeding tickets don't make you a wild child."

She didn't like that he dismissed it with that hmmph and raised eyebrow. Those tickets had really upset her parents and had caused her insurance to skyrocket. "Remember, I do have an ex-fiancé thief."

Egan shook his head. "That doesn't make you a wild child, either."

"My parents would disagree with you," she mumbled. And Caroline instantly regretted it. She didn't want to get into a discussion about how she felt she owed it to her parents to be a dutiful daughter.

"Your father had a pretty serious heart attack about the time your fiancé stole that money from him." Egan said it so nonchalantly that it took her a moment to realize the comment meant he'd had her investigated.

"Yes," Caroline admitted. "He nearly died. And please, spare me any psychoanalytical remarks about a guilty conscience."

"No comments." Egan tipped his head to the notebook still tucked beneath her arm. "That's your reconstructed dream journal?"

Oh, mercy. Another can of worms that she didn't want opened. "Yes. I'll give it to the psychiatrist tomorrow when I meet with her."

"*We'll* give it to her," Egan corrected, walking closer. He stopped just inches away.

"You're going to the appointment with me?" she asked.

"Actually, the appointment will be here at your house." He paused, studying her expression. "I shouldn't have to remind you that someone tried to kill you last night. I don't want you going out anywhere alone." He held out his hand. "Now, let me take a look at the journal."

Caroline had made up her mind to refuse, but she re-thought that. Because Egan would want to know why. She'd stall him, of course. Then he'd demand to know why she was stalling and refusing.

He'd see right through her.

Because he could.

And in the end, Egan would be suspicious, very suspicious, which would only make him examine every word of gibberish she'd written.

Since she had already lost the hypothetical argument she'd had with him, Caroline handed him the journal as calmly as she could and then went to take a closer look at one of the holes in her garage wall. She waited. While he read the single page.

"Killer clocks, huh?" he commented.

"It was a dream," she snapped. "It doesn't have to make sense."

She heard his footsteps, turned around, and he was there. Practically looming over her. He smelled…manly, with his woodsy, musky aftershave. Looked manly, too, with just the hint of bad-boy stubble on his strong chin.

"You think time's running out?" he asked, handing her back the journal.

"For what?" She sounded cautious. And was.

"For catching a killer," he answered as if that were the only possible answer.

"Yes. That's it." Good. No mention of phallic symbols or blond, blue-shirt-wearing Rangers, which meant Taylor had obviously been wrong.

"Holy moly," Egan mumbled.

Caroline was startled and then realized he wasn't looking at her or the journal, but rather he was looking past her. She followed his gaze to the open door of the workshop. From his angle he could no doubt see her *old secret.*

And he made a beeline for it.

Mercy! She tried to step in front of him. For all the good it did. He merely stepped around her. Caroline maneuvered again. Not very well. She finally gave up the maneuvering and latched onto Egan with both hands.

It wasn't a good idea.

The journal dropped to the floor, and her hands were suddenly filled with his left arm and right shoulder. But her attempts were useless, anyway. He saw her old secret.

"That's a mint condition vintage 1952 Harley-Davidson Panhead Chopper," he announced, studying the motorcycle. His mouth opened slightly, and she thought she saw the pulse in his neck rev up a little.

"So?" she challenged. "I bought it, as an investment. And it's a 1951, not a '52."

He didn't react to the correction. "Not a dent, not one rust spot, not even a paint chip. So, you've obviously taken good care of it. You actually ride it?"

Caroline clutched her heart necklace. "Sometimes." But only at night. When her parents were out of town. They considered anything with two wheels to be dangerous.

"When's the last time you took it out?" he asked, still mesmerized by the motorcycle.

She cleared her throat. "A week ago."

Egan shifted those scorching blue eyes in her direction, and the corner of his mouth hitched into a smile. "Now, owning *that* beauty makes you a wild child."

For some reason, a stupid one, that sounded, well, hot coming from him. That smile helped. Heck, who was she kidding? That smile alone had no doubt seduced countless women because that smile created a too-familiar tug in her belly.

Something stirred between them.

It was followed by a long smoldering look. Oh, the things those eyes were conveying. The Chopper had obviously revved up more than just his pulse and his admiration for her wild-child label.

Thankfully, he must have remembered their too-close

situation because the smile faded until all that was left was the surliness.

He stepped back.

She let go of him and stepped back, too.

"*This* is not going to be a problem between us," Egan said like a general issuing an order to one of his lieutenants.

Caroline bypassed a clarification of *this* mainly because she didn't want it spelled out. "It won't be a problem. Because I'll stay with my friend, Taylor, until you have this killer behind bars. We won't have to be around each other, if at all."

Egan shook his head. "If you stay with Taylor, basically you'll be bringing the danger right to her doorstep, because I think the killer will definitely try to come after you again. And I don't think he'll care if he has to go through your friend to get to you."

Oh, God. Caroline hadn't even considered that. She *had* thought of hiring a security guard, though. But what if that wasn't enough? What if the intruder returned, and this time what if Taylor got hurt?

Caroline couldn't bear the thought of that happening.

"Well," she said, not knowing what else to say. She'd have to come up with a plan, of course. Caroline just wished the fatigue fog in her head would go away so she could think more clearly.

"San Antonio CSI confirmed that last night someone intentionally cut your phone line," Egan said, his voice calm and even. "The footprints on your bedroom floor also prove someone entered your house through your bedroom door. The person who did that had to have some familiarity with the layout of your place. He only took one thing, your dream journal, and he apparently knew exactly where to find it."

"I already know all of this," she said, frustrated. And scared.

"Yeah. But have you figured out that the shrink appointment tomorrow afternoon is no doubt going to make this guy come after you again?"

No, she hadn't. But it would have occurred to her soon enough. "So, what am I to do? Give up? Hide? Run? Because I'm a little short of solutions here, and I obviously have a massive problem."

"Brody called earlier with the solution." Egan let that hang there between them for several seconds, and she could tell from the tense muscles in his jaw that it was not a solution either of them would like.

"I'm listening," Caroline said, while trying to brace herself.

"Brody wants you in protective custody. *My* protective custody. You got a guest room, wild child? I sure hope so because I'm moving in with you."

Chapter Five

Egan tried to ignore the fancy feminine surroundings and instead forced himself to concentrate on the surveillance video he'd gotten from the manager of the Cantara Hills Country Club restaurant.

On the screen of his laptop, Egan watched the images of Caroline having lunch with her parents and the Suttons. There was no audio, so he studied the body language.

Nothing seemed out of order.

Neither Tammy nor Kenneth was exhibiting any suspicious or unusual behavior. They appeared to be enjoying a casual lunch with friends. But that was just the surface. Caroline had talked about her dream journal that day, and he watched, waiting for a reaction to that. If he got a reaction, any reaction, he'd have to send the surveillance disk to the crime lab so a lip reader could examine it. He might have to do that anyway unless he got a solid lead.

He heard Caroline's footsteps coming down the hall toward him, and a moment later, she appeared in the doorway. Barefooted. She had her shoulder-length hair scooped up off her neck and held precariously in place with a clip.

She still wore the pale yellow skirt and top she'd put on earlier when CSI had given her the all-clear to move back into her house. The top clung to her breasts. And the skirt skimmed her thighs and butt.

And how did he know this bit of fashion information?

Because he was brainless and couldn't seem to stop himself from gawking at her.

As usual, she looked uncomfortable being around him. She'd looked that way the entire day, even though Egan had tried to keep his distance. It was a big house, but it still felt like close quarters despite the fact that Caroline had spent most of the time working in her office. It was just up the hall from the guest suite that he'd be using as his office and bedroom until Brody could make other arrangements.

Egan intended to make sure those other arrangements happened *soon*.

"Find anything on that surveillance tape?" She had a cut crystal glass of garnet-red wine in her hand.

He shook his head and closed the box of pizza he'd had delivered earlier. "It'd be nice if I had audio."

"Well, maybe I can help." She strolled toward him, across the white rugs. Yes, white. The large bedroom and sitting area were blue for the most part, but the navy-colored glossy hardwood floor was dotted with a trio of white rugs that seemed to be made out of bleached raw cotton. "After all, I was there. Maybe I can fill you in on what was being said."

She stood behind the translucent ice-blue acrylic desk where he was seated. The desk was small and dainty, barely three feet across and had just enough room for his pizza box, laptop and a few papers. The chair, too, was dainty and definitely not a comfortable fit for his butt and back.

"Oh," she commented, looking at the screen.

When she didn't say more, Egan stared up at her. "Care to explain that *oh?*"

"That's Miles Landis, Taylor's half brother, standing at the bar. He's a freeloader so most people steer clear of him. That's why he's sitting alone. I didn't know he was there that early. I didn't think he came in until we were nearly finished with lunch."

He'd already noticed the guy. Lanky and with three shades of unnatural color—one of them purple—in his trendy chopped hair.

Egan also hadn't missed his own father, who'd dropped in for a short conversation with Link Hathaway, the sixty-something business tycoon and his father's long-time employer. Link's daughter, Margaret, was there as well. The two were at the table next to Caroline's during the entire lunch and could have easily heard everything she'd said about the appointment with the shrink and the dream journal.

"Do you have any reason to believe Link Hathaway could have something to do with the murders?" Egan asked.

"No." Then she shrugged. "Well, only because I don't want to suspect any of my neighbors. But you probably already know since your father works for him that Link can be ruthless, both in business and in his personal life. He's ruled Margaret with an iron fist."

And his father, Walt, had no doubt helped Link rule with that ruthless, iron fist. Egan didn't know if his father had ever done anything illegal for Link, but maybe it was time to dig deeper.

His attention shifted to the delicate-looking blonde across from Link. Link's daughter, Margaret. Egan had seen her a couple of times when he was a kid, on those rare occasions when his father had taken him out to the Hathaway estate.

"Margaret Hathaway is forty-five," Egan supplied. "She must not mind her daddy's iron fist or else she wouldn't be having lunch with him."

"It wasn't a pleasant lunch," Caroline explained. She shook her head. "They argued. In whispers, but it was still an argument."

It probably wasn't important, but Egan's training and instincts made him want to know more. "What was the argument about?"

She blew out her breath. "This isn't common knowledge, and I'd like to keep it quiet for Margaret's sake. But years ago, she had a baby out of wedlock, and from what I've heard Margaret say, Link forced her to give up the little boy for adoption."

That definitely hadn't come up in the background check, nor had he heard his father ever mention it, which meant it'd been hidden or perhaps even removed from public records. "How long ago was this?"

"About thirty years or so. Margaret was just fifteen or sixteen when it happened."

So, her son would be about Egan's own age, although it probably wasn't significant. He did wonder why they'd be arguing about it now, but he had no evidence to suggest that Margaret Hathaway or her illegitimate child had anything to do with this. In fact, in the background checks Margaret was one of the few residents of Cantara Hills who'd come up squeaky-clean. Besides, Egan had a personal angle on this—Margaret had always been nice to him. Unlike her father.

And unlike Egan's own dad.

Movement on the screen snared his attention, and Egan spotted someone else he recognized.

"Carlson Woodward. He's the tennis pro at the country club," Caroline provided, pointing to the dark-haired man who'd just walked into the restaurant. He wore his athletic clothes and carried a leather bag over his shoulder. "Rumor has it that you have a history with him."

"Oh, yeah." And he wasn't surprised that info had gotten around. "Carlson, Brody, Hayes and I all grew up in the same neighborhood."

She made a sound of agreement, indicating she knew that. "Carlson *really* dislikes you."

"Well, I *really* dislike him. He's a twit." And Carlson had made Egan's life hell when they were growing up. Always tattling. Always scheming to get Egan into trouble. Always picking fights.

"Carlson seems jealous of you," Caroline added.

It was such a simple statement, but it gave Egan a new angle to look at this. Carlson was close enough to the table to have heard Caroline's conversation about the dream journal and the therapy appointment, and that meant Carlson could have repeated it to any and everyone.

Including the killer.

"What happened between Carlson and you to cause all this friction?" she asked.

He frowned at her question. "Too much happened."

"There must have been something to start it all."

His frown deepened. But since it wasn't anything secret and since Caroline apparently wanted to dig up old dirt, Egan cooperated while he watched the surveillance disk. "He stole something from me. A golden Lab puppy that Margaret Hathaway had given to me for my eighth birthday."

"He stole a puppy?" She sounded as outraged as Egan still felt about it.

"Stole him and hid him. Carlson locked him in a shed without any food or water and then demanded a ransom. If I didn't pay him twenty bucks, he was going to let the puppy die. I didn't have *one* dollar, much less twenty."

"You're right. He's a twit." Her forehead bunched up. "Please tell me you got the puppy back?"

"Oh, yeah." After he'd beaten the crud out of Carlson, forcing him to confess where he'd hidden the dog. Egan had gotten in bad trouble with his dad when Carlson had gone tattling to his parents, but it'd been worth it.

Because he wasn't enjoying this trip down memory lane, Egan focused on the screen. But that was it as far as surveillance. The end of the lunch. Caroline and her parents stood from the table. So did the Suttons. Hugs were exchanged all the way around, Caroline's father signed the bill and the five dispersed, walking out of camera range.

"I'm sorry Carlson did that to you," she said, her voice practically a whisper.

"So am I." And he was even sorrier that he'd told her the story. It wasn't a good connection for them to have.

Frustrated with himself and frustrated that he hadn't gotten more from the surveillance tape, Egan clicked it off. He was missing something. He was sure of it.

But what?

"What about the shoe search?" she asked, propping her right butt cheek on the corner of the desk.

Although it wasn't necessary, Egan looked at his notes.

It was better than looking at Caroline, who was now so close that he could touch her. And smell her. The woman knew how to make subtle scents work for her. "Kenneth does indeed wear a size ten shoe. Tammy, a perfect size six. Just as she said. The intruder wore a size eleven."

"So, it's a dead end." She set aside her wine, lifted the pizza box and looked inside.

"Help yourself," Egan said.

However, she'd already declined once when he'd offered to share it with her when it was first delivered. Instead, she insisted she would eat a deli-packaged fruit salad she'd taken from her fridge.

"I'm supposed to be eating healthier," she commented. "Family history of high cholesterol and such." But she didn't refuse now. Caroline took out a slice of the sausage and pepperoni and bit into it. She made a sound of pure pleasure.

A sound that hit him hard below the belt.

Get your mind back on business.

"What about your dream journal?" he asked. "Were you able to remember anything else to write in it?"

She nodded and then held up her index finger in a wait-a-second gesture. Caroline ate a hefty bite of the pizza and washed it down with her wine. "Not much. I remembered a dream about driving fast with the wind in my hair. Nothing about Kimberly, though, and that night."

He thought about it a moment. "Well, you were in car that night. A convertible. So, there would have been wind in your hair."

As if she'd suddenly lost her appetite, she put the remainder of the pizza slice back in the box and closed it. "Yes. It was a blue convertible." She paused. "The last thing I remember about that night was getting dressed for the party. That's it. And afterward…" She paused again. "I woke up in the hospital, and the only memories I have of those lost eight hours are what people have told me."

Caroline stared at him. "You don't believe me."

Egan hadn't expected the blatant accusation. "No." But he immediately shook his head. "Wait, I didn't mean that exactly. I don't think you're lying." And he hoped to hell his change of opinion had nothing to do with her great-fitting skirt and hot legs. "But I do think you're scared of learning the truth."

Caroline didn't say anything for several long seconds. "I *am* scared. Those six speeding tickets keep coming back to haunt me. And I hope I didn't do anything to contribute to what happened."

So did Egan, but he kept that to himself. He also resisted the urge to reach up and wipe the dab of pizza sauce from the corner of her mouth.

"From all accounts, Montoya was waiting for your car, waiting to kill. Maybe both of you. Maybe just Kimberly McQuade," he reminded her. "I don't think speeding would have helped or prevented him from doing what he'd set out to do. And my guess is the only reason you're alive is because you had on a seat belt. Kimberly didn't. And because you were unconscious, that saved your life. I think Montoya might have killed you, too, if you'd seen what he did."

"Maybe I did see," she whispered.

He looked up, caught her gaze, just as a tear streaked down her cheek. She quickly swiped it away and got up. She was halfway to the door before he made it out of that dainty chair and caught up with her.

Egan caught on to her arm and whirled her around to

face him. There it was again. That punch. That feeling of lust so deep that he had to release the grip on her. Touching her was just plain dangerous.

"Sorry about that," she mumbled.

Surprised, he shook his head. "About crying?"

"Yes. You don't need that. And I wasn't looking for pity."

"Good. Because I wouldn't have given you any. I'm not very good at providing pity."

She gave a choppy nod and turn to leave again.

"Caroline, there's a, uh, strict rule about Rangers getting personally involved with someone in their protective custody."

He didn't touch her.

But she stopped.

"Yes. I figured there would be. It's just as well. I couldn't get involved with you anyway." She frowned. "Don't look at me like that. It doesn't have anything to do with your being a chauffeur's son. It's just I can't do anything else to upset my father. I love him more than life itself, but he can be a snob. He thinks my only path to happiness is for me to be with what he calls 'my own kind.'"

None of this surprised Egan, but for some reason, it riled him. How was this any different from Link Hathaway's ruling his daughter's life? A powerful, rich daddy trying to manipulate his family's gene pool. "So, what does that mean—you marry some guy of your father's choosing?"

Caroline smugly lifted her shoulder and her chin. "Who says I have to marry at all?"

He saw it then. That defiance that went bone-deep. It wasn't just in her silky voice but in her body language.

Yeah. She'd been a wild child, and that rich, polished demeanor barely disguised it.

"You're smiling," she commented.

Hell. He quickly changed his expression.

Egan went closer, and because it was driving him crazy, he reached out and skimmed his thumb over the corner of her mouth to get that pizza sauce.

Except it turned into something else.

Caroline, obviously not realizing what he was trying to do, moved. It caused his thumb to slide over her bottom lip. Her breath shivered a bit and brushed against his thumb. It was a heated moment that Egan felt in every inch of his body.

Before he pulled back his hand.

And cursed.

She cursed, too.

What they didn't do was move away from each other. Bad idea. Really bad. Because his primed body came up with a suggestion as to what to do about that closeness, and about that shiver in her breath.

The doorbell rang.

Thank God.

But then Egan remembered it was well past 10 p.m. Hardly the hour for visitors. And with the killer on the loose, he instantly went on alert.

"Expecting anyone?" he asked Caroline.

When she shook her head, he withdrew his service pistol from his shoulder holster and made his way to the front door. Caroline was right behind him, but he motioned for her to stand back.

The bell rang again. Not just once. But a series of frantic jabs, followed by a heavy-handed knock.

"Caroline!" the visitor shouted. "It's me, Miles. I need to talk to you. It's important."

Miles Landis. The half brother of Caroline's best friend, Taylor. "Any idea what he wants?" Egan asked Caroline.

"No. Maybe," she amended. She crossed the room and reached for the doorknob, but Egan stopped her. Catching on to her arm, he positioned her on the other side of a large plant, and after he'd made sure that she was out of the line of fire, Egan disengaged the security system and opened the door.

Miles Landis had his fist poised for another knock but quickly withdrew his hand. The man looked disheveled, but Egan didn't know if it was because Miles was making some kind of a fashion statement or if this was an emergency visit.

"I need to speak with Caroline," Miles insisted.

"About what?"

Miles dodged eye contact with Egan. "It's personal."

"He's here to ask me for a loan," Caroline provided.

Apparently following the sound of her voice, Miles tried to stick his head inside, but Egan blocked him from doing that. However, he heard Caroline walk closer, and she didn't stop until she was right at Egan's shoulder.

"The answer is no," she told Miles. "I won't give you another loan. And neither will Taylor."

Miles swallowed hard, and if a person could smell as though he was desperate, this guy had accomplished it. "I wouldn't have come if it weren't important. I need money, Caroline, and you know you wouldn't miss it with your bank account."

She folded her arms over her chest. "That won't work with me. Taylor and I have talked about this, and we agreed no more bailing you out of sticky situations. Go home, Miles. Stop gambling and you won't need to hit up your friends and family for loans."

Egan knew from the background check that Miles had major financial problems. What he didn't know about were these loan requests.

Something flashed in Miles's eyes. A strong mixture of emotions. Disappointment. Fear. And even anger. *Nope*—make that rage. Miles was one pissed-off guy.

And that made Egan look down at the guy's feet.

"What size shoes do you wear?" Egan asked.

Some of the rage faded, replaced by what Egan thought might be amusement. "Size eleven. Why, is that the size Caroline's intruder wore? I heard rumors that the crime scene guys found some tracks."

Egan didn't verify that. Instead, he took out his cell phone and called his fellow Ranger, Hayes, who was at the office at the country club.

"Hayes, we need a search warrant, fast," Egan instructed. "And have SAPD go over to Miles Landis's condo. Mr. Landis won't be allowed in until the place has been searched. Specifically, we're looking for his size eleven athletic shoes."

"I take it this Landis is a possible match to those tracks left on Caroline's floor?" Hayes asked.

"Oh, yes." Well, in the shoe department, anyway. Since only the dream journal had been stolen, this hard-up-for-money guy obviously hadn't broken in to get stuff to sell for his much-needed loan.

But then, maybe Miles intended to sell that dream journal to someone.

"There's some good news and bad news on those shoe

prints," Hayes let him know. "The tread indicates that the shoes are Razors. That's a fairly new brand name and an expensive one, so only a few people should have them. They're mainly tennis shoes."

"Interesting." And Egan knew they were both wondering if this was connected to their old nemesis, Carlson Woodward. After all, Carlson was a tennis pro at the country club and had easy access to of any part Cantara Hills. Plus, he knew all the victims. "What's the bad news?"

"It's possible that the person wearing those Razors isn't a size eleven. The CSI guys say there's something off with the pressure points of the tracks. Either the intruder could have been wearing shoes that were too big or the person was just walking funny."

"What does that mean?" But Egan already suspected what it meant, and if so, it wasn't good.

"Apparently, the guy could have purposely used the balls of his feet to throw off the way the soles landed on the floor. In other words, our intruder might or might not actually wear size eleven shoes."

And since the intruder had picked such an unusual brand of footwear, those shoe prints could have been made to encourage them to go after the wrong person. Was that break-in really just a setup to cast suspicion on someone else other than the real killer?

Miles smiled when Egan finished the call and slipped his phone back into his pocket. "Get your warrant, Sgt. Caldwell, but I don't have anything to hide. I don't have the kind of shoes you're trying to match."

Egan shrugged. "How do you know what I'm trying to match?"

"I don't, but since I wasn't the one to break into Caroline's house, I couldn't have possibly left those tracks. Therefore, I don't have the shoes you're looking for." He couldn't have sounded more arrogant if he'd tried.

Egan returned the arrogant attitude. "But you won't be offended if I don't take your word for it." He shut the door in the man's face, locked it and used the keypad on the wall to reengage the entire security system. Earlier, Egan had already checked all the doors and windows to make sure they were locked. He'd check them again before heading off to bed.

Still, even with all the precautions, it was going to be a long, restless night.

For a lot of reasons.

"What bad news did Hayes tell you?" Caroline wanted to know.

He stopped there in the foyer and looked at her. "The intruder might have worn bigger shoes to throw off the track marks."

"Oh. So this doesn't let Kenneth off the hook."

"It doesn't let anyone off the hook." Egan tipped his head to the door where their visitor had just been. "Do you think Miles could have stolen the dream journal with maybe the idea to blackmail you with it?"

She shrugged. "I guess that's possible. But that leaves the bomb. I don't know of any reason why Miles would want me dead."

Neither did Egan, but that didn't mean there wasn't one. Miles was a desperate man, and desperate men often did dangerous things.

And speaking of dangerous things…

There was a problem that Caroline and he hadn't discussed yet. Best to get it over with. Like ripping off a bandage.

"I need to modify the sleeping arrangements," he told her. "Your bedroom is on the other side of the house from the guest suite. Plus, there are those two French doors in your room that would give an intruder easy access."

She pointed to the keypad, where he'd just punched in the code. "But the security system is on."

"True. But this person's already cut a phone line and tampered with your old security system. I can't take the chance of not being able to hear you if something goes wrong."

He watched that register in the depths of those blue-green eyes. It didn't register well, especially after that pizza sauce–wiping incident. All that mouth touching had created a weird sort of intimacy that neither needed.

"What exactly did you have in mind?" Caroline asked cautiously.

Egan tried not to think of what he really had on his mind. Sex on the foyer floor wasn't going to happen despite his body's insistence that it should.

"The guest suite where I'm staying has fewer windows and no outside access. It's the room that'd be the easiest to monitor and secure." He hoped the next part didn't sound as troubling as he thought it would. "You take the bed. And I'll take the floor."

Caroline blinked. "You want *us* to sleep in the same room?"

He nodded, hoping that it looked authoritative and confident, and then Egan put his hand on the small of her back to get her moving in the direction of the guest suite.

"You *really* think this is a good idea?" she asked. Apparently, he'd failed at looking confident.

"No," he admitted. But sleeping in the same room was better than the alternative of not being able to protect her if something went wrong. Egan planned to do whatever it took to keep Caroline alive.

That included spending the night just a few feet away from her with all those hot images of raunchy floor sex scorching his body.

Man, he wanted her bad.

Chapter Six

Caroline dreamed.

The images were spliced together like fragments from a half-dozen different situations. She was in the car, wind in her hair. And it was dark. She had the feeling that someone was seated next to her.

A woman.

Caroline tried to turn her head to see who the woman was, but she couldn't. She could hear only two words. *Seat belt.* The words pounded in her head, repeating themselves over and over until they became painful.

Then the scene changed. Different images. The clocks were after her again. Not some cute timepieces. These clocks had fangs and had removed their hands to use as spears, which they hurled at her.

She ran. So fast. So hard. Until she thought her heart might explode. And the man came and began shooting arrows. The arrows worked because the clocks retreated.

Then the man kissed her.

That kiss relaxed her. Just like that. Fear faded from her mind, and in its place was the slow, hungry sensation of being seduced. He took off her clothes. Not in some hurried frenzy but gently, as if time didn't matter.

But it didn't last. Things changed again. Someone was calling out her name, and someone had hold of her. Not in a seducing kind of way, either. This person's grip was frantic. The danger had returned. She wasn't safe.

Caroline fought to release herself from the grip. She punched at the person. Not once—several times, but she couldn't break the hold he had on her.

"Caroline!" he said. "Wake up!"

And his command was clear. *Very* clear.

She forced open her eyes and realized why it was so clear. Because Egan had indeed said her name. He was still saying it, and he had hold of her hands. And she wasn't exactly cooperating. She was thrashing and trying to kick him. Obviously, she'd gotten caught up in the dream.

But why was Egan there…in bed with her? And there was no doubt about that. In the moonlit room, Caroline had no trouble seeing him. He had her practically pinned to the mattress.

"Wake up!" Egan insisted, sounding frustrated and in pain.

Caroline was in pain, too. Her right fist was stinging, and it took her a moment to figure out why. She replayed the last moments of that "dream" and figured out what she might have done.

She quit thrashing and fighting and went limp. "God, did I hit you?"

"Yeah, you did." Huffing, Egan rolled off her and landed on his back next to her. His breath was coming out in rough, short bursts. "You hit like a girl," he grumbled. "Well, except for that last punch." He rubbed the right side of his jaw and winced.

She fought through the haze left by the dream and got hit with a full dose of reality. "I hurt you."

And that wasn't all she'd done.

She'd put on pj's for bed. Her most matronly pair—cotton, at that—but the top was now shoved up high, and her bare breasts were exposed. Caroline quickly tried to right it, but she had, no doubt, given Egan an eyeful.

Speaking of eyefuls, she looked at him. And got one, too. He was naked. Well, from the waist up, anyway. Shirtless, he lay there, obviously trying to gather his breath, while the moonlight bathed over him. What a vision. All those toned and tanned pecs. Washboard abs. Of course. But that wasn't the best part. The best part was that he'd removed his belt, and his jeans had dipped down low on his hips.

Very low.

There was a thin strip of hair that led from his navel right down into his jeans, where there was an eye-catching bulge that made her go hot all over.

Mercy.

She couldn't want him this much. Or even half this much. But Caroline couldn't deny that her body was suddenly warm and wet in a place it shouldn't have been. Her breasts began to tingle, and she felt her nipples tighten. That tug in her belly became a hard pull.

This was *so* not going to happen.

"I'm never going to admit you hurt me with that last punch," Egan said, his voice not much more than a growl. That turned her on, too. "So let's get past it so I can tell you why I tried to wake you up. It's because you were talking in your sleep."

That didn't turn her on. Just the opposite. "Was I?"

Good grief. "What did I say?" *And please no melting kisses or clothing removal. No sex stuff at all.*

"You kept saying 'seat belt' and that you'd hit your head."

Okay. She nodded. Caroline remembered the seat belt but not the head part. "I think I was dreaming about that night of the hit-and-run."

"I thought so, too. I figured if I woke you up, the dream would still be fresh, and you might recall something."

Did she? Caroline sat up and turned on the lamp next to the bed. Just on the other side of that on the floor was Egan's crumpled sleeping bag, which he'd obviously vacated in a hurry.

"Seat belt," she repeated. There was something, but it was just out of reach. She closed her eyes, concentrated hard, and it just wouldn't come. "I'm sorry."

He continued to stare at the ceiling. "What about your head? Do you remember why it was hurting?"

"No. I only remember that it was hurting because I kept hearing the words *seat belt*. I'm sorry."

"Don't be. It was a long shot." He got up off the bed and walked toward his sleeping bag. He rubbed his back. Perhaps because he was sore from sleeping on the floor. Or maybe she'd injured him there in the struggle.

He stopped by her side of the bed, looked down and reached for her neck. For a moment, one body-warming moment, she thought he was going to touch her. But he didn't. Instead, he touched the collar of her pj's and pulled something from it. She heard a soft pop.

"The price tag," he said, dropping it onto the nightstand. "I guess you don't wear those very often."

"No. I usually—" Thank heaven she didn't finish that.

"Sleep commando?" he finished for her.

Caroline's mouth dropped open. How the heck had he figured that out?

"You have very smooth sheets," he said as if anticipating her question. "They feel damn good on bare skin." He shrugged. "Plus, it's how any wild child, former or otherwise, sleeps."

So, that meant he slept naked, too. Caroline didn't ask him to confirm it.

But she could envision it.

"Get some rest," he insisted, returning to the sleeping bag. She watched him climb in and got a great view of his butt. The man was delicious eye candy.

She turned off the light, lay back on her pillow and closed her eyes. She had to get her mind off Egan. Better to think about the dream instead. So that's what she did as she tried to drift back to sleep.

Caroline saw it then. The fringes of the dream that she hadn't been able to focus in on before.

"Seat belt," she mumbled.

She heard Egan sit back up, but she didn't look at him for fear that the murky image would go away.

"Kimberly is upset about something," she said, repeating what she saw in her head. "And she's not wearing her seat belt. I tell her to put it on. She's reaching for it…and that's it." Caroline slowly opened her eyes and glanced at Egan. "I'm sorry, but that's all I can see."

"Kimberly didn't have on the seat belt when Montoya hit your car," Egan reminded her. "So that must have happened just seconds before impact."

That made sense. "Maybe this means I'm regaining my memory."

"Maybe. And maybe the new drug the shrink's giving you tomorrow will make you remember everything."

Yes.

Everything.

Caroline only hoped that whatever she'd done, or hadn't done, she would be able to live with it. But she was terrified that she was the one responsible for killing Kimberly McQuade.

"THIS IS A NEW BARBITURATE drug," Dr. Elsa Whitaker explained to Caroline and Egan. "Fast acting. Ultra, we call it. Caroline, you should go under quickly, within minutes, and you'll only be out for a half hour tops. I'm aiming for fifteen minutes. That seems to be the optimum range for the effectiveness of this drug."

So, since it was 3:00 p.m., that meant by three-fifteen, Egan might finally have some answers about that night when all these murders had started.

Caroline was already lying on the white leather sofa in her living room. She was barefoot, dressed in jeans and a loose green top, and she had several pillows tucked beneath her head. The phones had been silenced, and there was a Do Not Disturb sign on the door. In short, everything was ready to get this show on the road.

"And you're positive the drug is safe?" Egan asked.

Dr. Whitaker flexed her dark eyebrows. "As safe as any drug like this can be."

Yes. Dr. Whitaker had already explained that to Brody and him when they'd first brought up the idea. Safety hadn't seemed as much of a concern then as it did now. "Could you go over those safety issues again?" Egan requested.

"Of course. The drug has been tested on nearly a

hundred people, with the only side effect being a temporary headache, followed by fatigue. Also temporary." The doctor volleyed glances at both of them. "This is the best drug for this session. I've gone through Caroline's records, and she's already had hypnosis, therapy, and her therapist even administered the more traditional drug, thiopental. If you want these memories recalled, then this is our best bet."

"Let's do it," Caroline insisted.

But the doctor didn't move until Egan gave the nod.

Egan hoped he wouldn't regret this.

He watched as the doctor gave Caroline the injection. She winced a little and looked over at him. He could see the worry in her eyes. He was worried, too. Worried that this was all for nothing and worried they might learn something that would be too hard to hear.

He didn't even want to vocalize what "too hard to hear" might entail.

Dr. Whitaker was a tall woman, over six feet, and she had the wide shoulders and hips to go with that height. However, her face was gentle, and she spoke in soft whispers. Egan hoped that kind voice would make Caroline feel at ease.

Because he sure didn't.

He had the tape recorder in his hand, and he knew once Caroline was under and talking, he'd have to start recording. A recording that would be dissected by not only himself but Hayes, Brody and God only knew how many other Rangers and law enforcement officials.

Which brought him to something he needed to clarify.

"There's no need to ask her any questions about her previous personal relationships," Egan told the doctor. "It isn't pertinent to the case."

That earned him a questioning raised eyebrow from Dr. Whitaker and a puzzled look from Caroline. "Thank you," she mouthed.

He wasn't doing this for Caroline, Egan told himself. But the problem was, he couldn't figure out why he was doing it. Still, there was no reason for the world to know about Caroline's thieving ex-fiancé.

Dr. Whitaker sat in the chair next to Caroline's head, and after the fifteen minutes had passed, Egan turned on the recorder.

"I read your dream journal, Caroline." The doctor picked up the notebook from the granite-and-steel coffee table and glanced through it again. "You have a lot of things going on. I'd say there's some anxiety about your future. Maybe biological clock issues. And then there are the phallic symbols. All of these are perfectly natural for a young woman like you."

Phallic symbols?

Egan glanced at Caroline to see if she could clarify, but her eyelids were already fluttering down.

"Caroline, let's talk about the seat belt dream, the one you had last night," the doctor continued. "Go back into that dream for me. Can you do that?"

Caroline gave a wobbly nod.

"Good. Think about the dream and what happened with the hit-and-run. Talk to me about Kimberly McQuade. You're driving from your friend Taylor's house. You're in your car. It's night, and even though it's December, it's unseasonably warm. Do you remember all of that?"

Egan held his breath until Caroline nodded again.

"That's good, Caroline. Keep thinking about that night,"

Dr. Whitaker instructed. "Think about what you were doing. You said Kimberly is upset. Why is she upset?"

Caroline didn't answer right away, and she mumbled something indistinguishable before she finally spoke. "She's had an argument with Kenneth at the party. She wants to leave, but her car isn't there so she asks me to take her back to her apartment. We get in my car, and we leave."

"What did Kenneth and Kimberly argue about?" Egan immediately asked.

But the doctor frowned and put her finger to her mouth to indicate he needed to stay quiet.

"Did Kimberly tell you about the argument with Kenneth?" the doctor said to Caroline.

"In a way. We're in the car, and she says she's, uh, disappointed and angry. But she won't tell me why. She says she's going to look into the matter further."

Egan motioned for Dr. Whitaker to jump on that, and she did. "Did Kimberly tell Kenneth, too, that she was going to look into the matter?"

"Yes." The answer came fast, with no shred of doubt. "She says that's when he got angry with her. He threatened her. She wanted to leave the party after that."

Hell. That was motive. But Egan still didn't know what had caused the argument. He needed more pieces of this puzzle.

He hurried to the sofa and used a blank page in the dream journal to scribble down the next question. "How did Kenneth threaten Kimberly?" the doctor read aloud.

"I don't know." Caroline shook her head. "Kimberly's not saying."

The doctor and Egan shared a look of frustration. "Did Kimberly say anything else about Kenneth?"

Caroline's forehead bunched up. "No. She doesn't want to talk about him because she's so upset." She hesitated. "Kimberly wipes some tears from her cheek. And I notice that she's not wearing her seat belt. 'You need to put on the seat belt,' I tell her."

Egan could almost see it. Brody's little sister's last moments of life.

"Kimberly tries to put on the seat belt," Caroline continued. "But it's stuck. So I reach over to help her, but the belt's caught in the door. I need to pull over, so I slow down and look for a place to stop. I can't stop in the road. It's too dangerous. Someone coming over that hill wouldn't see us."

Caroline's expression changed. Her face was no longer relaxed, and he could see her eyes moving frantically beneath her lids.

"What's happening, Caroline?" the doctor asked.

She swallowed hard. "There's a car. Just a blink of an eye. And it's there. From a side street. It comes at us so fast." She began to shake. "It's there. It's there. God, it's there!"

Egan walked toward her, but the doctor waved him off. Instead, she laid her hand on Caroline's arm and rubbed gently. "It's all right. You're safe." She waited a moment until Caroline quit repeating those two words, *it's there*.

Egan would remember those words and that pain on her face for a long, long time.

"Did you see the driver of the other car?" the doctor continued.

Caroline shook her head. "No. Too fast. The car was there, and then everything went black."

"Because your head hit the steering wheel. Did you feel it when you hit your head?"

Caroline didn't answer right away. "A second of pain. Then, nothing."

Egan had been afraid of that. If Caroline was unconscious, and she likely was at this point of the hit-and-run, then even the drug wouldn't be able to uncover what had happened during those critical moments.

"What about sounds?" the doctor pressed. "Footsteps? Someone's voice?"

"I don't hear Kimberly. And not footsteps—" She stopped. "But I hear a sound. There's another car coming."

Yes. Another car had indeed come, and the driver had been Gary Zelke, who'd sideswiped Caroline's car, possibly even contributing to her injuries. Of course, Gary wasn't around any longer to question about that since he'd been murdered.

Caroline's eyelids fluttered, and the doctor looked back at Egan. "She's not going to be under much longer. Is there anything else you want me to ask her?"

"I want to know more about what Kimberly said to her." Egan was going on gut instinct here, but his first thought about what could have caused that argument was something he hadn't considered before. "Ask her if Kimberly was having an affair with Kenneth."

Dr. Whitaker looked even less comfortable with the question than Egan did. "Caroline, leave the accident and go back to the party. Kimberly and Kenneth have argued, and Kimberly's upset. Did she tell you anything about having an affair—"

"Yes," Caroline interrupted. "We talked about that. I was a little distraught. I'd heard gossip at the party. Gossip about my ex-fiancé. I went to the bathroom, and Kimberly was there outside the door. She asked what was wrong with me, and I told her I was having guy troubles. She laughed. Said she was having guy troubles, too—an affair. But it was complicated. She didn't want anyone to know until she'd sorted it all out."

Egan couldn't stop himself from asking the next question. "Was the affair with Kenneth?"

"No." She frowned. "I mean, I don't know. Kimberly didn't say, and I didn't ask."

So…Kimberly had been having a secret affair. And it was a secret. Well, from her brother at least. If Brody had known about it, he would have already told Egan. But now the real question was, was this some clue to discovering the identity of a killer?

It was if her lover had been Kenneth.

Kenneth might have ordered his goon, Montoya, to murder Kimberly if she'd been about to expose the affair. Kenneth's wife, Tammy, didn't look the sort to forgive and forget such an indiscretion, and as a career politician, Kenneth would need his high society, rich wife by his side when he made his bid to be governor.

Caroline's eyes opened, and even though she obviously had trouble focusing, her gaze landed on Egan.

"Are you okay?" he asked.

She nodded. "I'm dizzy. And I have a mild headache. But I remember everything I said."

"Anything else you remember?" Dr. Whitaker pressed.

"No. I can see bits and pieces of the hit-and-run, and I can recall that conversation about the affair, but that's it." She tried to sit up, and that's when Egan saw her blink back the tears. "I didn't cause Kimberly's death. I slowed down. I tried to get her to put on her seat belt."

"Yes," Egan managed to say, but it was hard to speak

even that one word with the sudden lump in his throat. He could feel the emotional burden that Caroline had been carrying all these months.

Dr. Whitaker patted Caroline's hand. "You did great." And then she stood, facing Egan, and picked up her medical bag. "That's it for today. I can give her another dose but not for at least forty-eight hours."

Egan would have to talk to Caroline about another dose. He walked the doctor to the door. "She'll be okay?"

"From the drug—yes. But she might have trouble dealing with these memories. If she does, give me a call, and I can have someone bring over a mild sedative."

Alarmed, Egan turned off the recorder and set it on the foyer table. "You think that'll be necessary?"

"Never can tell how people will react when being confronted with trauma. Just don't leave her alone." She reached for the door and then stopped. "Oh, and it's possible she'll remember even more. You might want to brace yourself in case her dreams aren't dreams tonight but rather nightmares."

Hell. What had he gotten Caroline into?

"You know I don't want you to repeat anything Caroline said here today," Egan reminded her.

Dr. Whitaker nodded, said her goodbye and left. Egan locked the door behind her and engaged the security system.

"So, I might have nightmares," he heard Caroline say. "It's okay," she added before he could apologize. "It was worth it. It's a huge relief to remember that I didn't do anything to hurt Kimberly. And now we know about the argument with Kenneth."

Egan walked closer and looked at her. She was pale. And he suspected that her mild headache wasn't so mild.

He reached down and scooped her up into his arms.

Obviously shocked, she stared at him. "Where are you taking me?"

"To bed. No, not for that," he clarified when she gave him a puzzled look. "I want you to take a nap, and if your headache doesn't go away, I'll call the doctor and ask her what you should take for pain."

"Okay." She settled her head against his shoulder as if she completely trusted him.

Egan walked to the guest suite, placed her on the bed and draped the side of the comforter over her.

"Caroline, I don't want you to say anything to anyone about what you remembered."

"I didn't remember much," she insisted.

Egan silently disagreed. Caroline might have remembered just enough to get her killed.

Chapter Seven

Using the controls on the wall of the marble shower, Caroline adjusted the trio of showerheads to "deep massage" and let the steamy hot water go to work. The pressure felt good on her muscles, and mercy did she need it. That four-hour nap following the session had given her a foggy head and a stiff neck.

Still, those minor discomforts were worth it. She'd learned the truth.

Or at least part of the truth.

She hadn't caused the accident that'd killed Kimberly. It was a hollow victory, though, because obviously nothing would bring back the young woman, but Caroline thought she might finally be able to get a decent night's sleep.

Well, she might if she could quit thinking about the killer.

And about Egan.

This whole sexual thing she was feeling for him had to stop. He wasn't a scumbag criminal like her ex-fiancé, Julian, but Egan was equally dangerous in the sense that a relationship with him, even a purely sexual one, would cause her parents to worry. And the last time they'd *worried,* her father had nearly died of a heart attack.

So, no more sexual fantasies and dreams about Egan.

Besides, this was just a crazy crush or something. Temporary. Mostly one-sided. Certainly not based on anything with emotional substance. She wanted to sleep with him, that was it, and since that couldn't happen, she would just have to put him out of her mind.

Bolstered by her little lecture, Caroline finished the shower, dried off and dressed in her black jeans and her favorite comfortable top, a tomato-red sleeveless tee that stopped loose at her waist. She debated putting on some makeup. Opted against it. There wasn't any reason for her to look her best.

She opened the bathroom door.

And heard the voices.

Not friendly voices, either. Egan was obviously arguing with someone.

Alarmed, Caroline rushed through her bedroom, following the sound of those voices. It wasn't difficult. Because someone was shouting.

When she got to the foyer, she realized that someone was Link Hathaway. He wasn't alone, either. He was in the doorway with Kenneth, and Egan's father, Walt, and the men appeared to be trying to barge their way into her house.

Link wore his usual starched jeans and black leather jacket. Practically a uniform for him. And he also had on his usual semi-scowling expression. Caroline had never seen the man smile, and she'd known him her entire life.

Kenneth wasn't exactly smiling, either. He was aiming a venomous glare at Egan.

Wearing a real uniform for his job as a chauffeur, Walt stood behind the other two men, and even though Caroline had known of him for years, it was really the first time she'd ever looked at him. There were no traces of Egan in his face. His coloring was different with his gingerish hair and cold, steely eyes. Plus, he lacked Egan's air of authority. The only air that Walt seemed to have was one of indifference. Not for his boss. But for his own son.

"What's going on?" she demanded.

"I was about to shoot all three of them," Egan said drily. "Because I've asked them to leave, and they won't."

"We had to make sure you were okay," Kenneth volunteered, aiming a final glare at Egan. His expression softened a bit when it rested on her. "Your phone's turned off, and that Do Not Disturb sign has been on the door all afternoon. Tammy and I got worried."

"Sorry. But I was…resting." Best to leave it at that. "I'm fine. Nothing's wrong."

Kenneth studied her face and wet hair and gave her a look that hinted as if he might challenge her nothing's-wrong comment. "Tammy saw the strange car drive up to your house earlier and then she noticed the woman visitor who came to your door. We figured you'd had the appointment with the psychiatrist."

She had no idea how to answer that, but she didn't have to. Egan spoke up. "Caroline decided not to go through with the session."

Link and Kenneth exchanged a puzzling glance.

"We learned the drug's still experimental," Egan continued. "It was too risky. I'll just have to find the killer another way. Maybe through his shoes."

"I'm a size twelve," Link snarled when Egan looked in that direction. "And you aren't going to catch me wearing any half-assed tennis shoes. Besides, if I wanted somebody dead, I wouldn't go sneaking around in a woman's bedroom to do it. That's something only a coward would do."

Caroline believed him. But she was puzzled as to why Link and his chauffeur were there at her house. Link wasn't the sort to cower, or to personally check up on people. Well, other than his daughter, Margaret.

"Mr. Hathaway, Mr. Caldwell, why are you here?" Caroline just came out and asked.

Walt didn't utter a word, and Link's scowl intensified. "Your father called," Link explained. "He asked me to check on you. When I got here, Kenneth had just pulled up with plans to do the same. You got a lot of people worried about you, girl, but obviously you're all in one piece."

"Obviously. If my parents call again, please tell them there's no need to send anyone over to check on me. I'll tell them myself when I phone them tonight."

"Do that," Link snarled. "It'll save me from playing messenger." And he strolled away. Walt didn't even look at his son when he followed his boss.

Kenneth, however, didn't leave with them. "Caroline, why don't you come and stay with Tammy and me? Your parents would like that."

Again, Egan answered before she could. "She's in my protective custody," Egan reminded Kenneth. "And I doubt that invitation to stay at your house extends to me."

"No. It doesn't." Kenneth spared Egan another glance before returning his attention to Caroline. "Tammy and I are here for you. Call if you need anything."

"I will." She'd hardly gotten the words out of her mouth before Egan shut the door and locked it. He also rearmed the security system. "I'm sorry about that," she told him. "I obviously have protective neighbors."

"Or nosy ones." He kept watch out the sidelight window. "I made you a sandwich. It's in the kitchen. And I called Dr. Whitaker, and she said it was all right if you had a glass of wine. Or Oreos, whichever you prefer."

"Thanks. Oreos for dessert. But I'll start with the wine." Since she was starving, she headed for the kitchen. "Can I pour you a glass?"

"No. I'm on duty."

Of course he was. Sometimes, it was easy for her to forget that. Like when he was half-naked on her bed. But now, with his hand on the barrel of his gun and with his intense stare out the window at her departing guests, there was no doubt that this was *duty* for him.

"Did anybody else come by when I was napping?" she asked from the kitchen. The sandwich, ham and cheese on wheat, was waiting for her on the counter, but first she opened a bottle of pinot noir and poured herself a glass.

"Hayes came by. He picked up the recording of your session with the shrink, but I don't think he'll hear anything we didn't hear."

Caroline made a sound of agreement and sampled the sandwich. It was good, but then she was starving. She realized it was the first thing she'd eaten all day. She'd wanted to lose a few pounds, but this wasn't a diet she could recommend to anyone.

"I also got a call about the shoes that we took from Miles Landis's closet." Egan stopped in the doorway and bracketed his hands on both sides of the frame. The muscles in his arms and chest responded to the simple movement.

So did Caroline.

"Miles is definitely size eleven," Egan explained. "But

there was no match. Of course, he could have gotten rid of the shoes."

That was true of any of their suspects. "So, we still don't know who's trying to kill me."

"Well, we're pretty sure it's connected to Kimberly's death. Because the attempt to murder you didn't start until everyone heard that you were trying to regain your memory."

"Yes." Caroline groaned softly. "Something I regret broadcasting."

Egan shrugged. "You couldn't have known the consequences."

Nor could she know where it would end. That bomb had been designed to kill her. No doubt about that. But would Egan's lie that she'd changed her mind about taking the memory drug be enough to get the killer to back off? She ate more of the sandwich and contemplated that.

And then she noticed he was staring at her.

"What?" she asked.

Egan shook his head. And that didn't exactly seem to be a lustful look he was giving her. "What is it?" Caroline repeated.

"Nothing. It's just the pinot noir brings back some old memories."

She smiled. She liked this conversation better than the other. "What, memories of wild college parties?"

"No." He took his right hand from the frame and rubbed his forehead as if he'd regretted bringing this up. "When I was growing up, we used to live on the same street with an elderly woman who used to drink a lot of that particular kind of wine. I mean two or three bottles a day, and she'd pay my dad to get it for her since she couldn't drive. Because there were lots of times when my dad had other things to do, he made an arrangement with the seedy liquor store owner for me to be able to pick it up for her on my walk home from school."

Caroline's smile faded completely. "Good grief. How old were you?"

"It started when I was seven. Once, the bag broke, and I dropped one of the bottles on the way back to the house. Got in a whole boatload of trouble for that."

Caroline could only imagine, and it outraged her. "It's your father, the stupid store owner and your neighbor who should have gotten in trouble. They shouldn't have had a seven-year-old picking up alcohol."

He dismissed it with a shake of his head. "It was a long time ago."

She had a sudden desire to pour the rest of her wine down the drain, but that would be too obvious. Plus, she instinctively knew that would be even harder on Egan. It'd probably been a while since he'd discussed this with anyone, and he wouldn't want her to make a big deal of it.

"Why didn't your mother stop what was going on?" she asked.

"She left when I was just a baby. I figured that's why my dad hated me." He rubbed his forehead again, indicating a change of subject was on the way. "Brody and Victoria haven't had any luck finding the person they were looking for, so they're coming back from California tomorrow. I figure the three of us—Hayes, Brody and me—will take turns staying here."

The bite of the sandwich she took nearly lodged in her throat. "That makes sense, I guess."

He stared at her. "You think I'm doing that because I don't want to be around you."

She obviously hadn't hidden her emotions, or else he could read her well. "Isn't that why?"

"Yes." He didn't even hesitate, and he looked her straight in the eye when he said it.

That stung, more than she had imagined it would. Great. So much for her shower lecture about not getting involved with him. Caroline finished off her glass of wine, poured herself another one and walked closer to him so she could, well, start an argument or something. Anything was better than feeling the sting of his rejection. It, too, brought back old painful memories of her breakup with her ex-fiancé.

"Don't take it personally," Egan said, his voice low and husky. "This is my fault. I'm attracted to you."

Caroline stopped. Just a few inches away from him. And there was no argument to start because she couldn't think of what to say in response to that.

He was attracted to her?

Better yet, he was admitting it?

So, maybe it wasn't one-sided after all, and maybe it wasn't just her Harley that had him in a lather.

"And I shouldn't be attracted to you," Egan continued. "It's unprofessional and dangerous. There's a reason for the regulation about a Ranger not getting personally involved with someone in his protective custody. A personal involvement could cause me to lose focus. That could get you killed."

Caroline took a deep breath. Hearing it all spelled out that way, she couldn't disagree with him. He was right. If they were lusting after each other, then their focus wouldn't be on catching a killer.

Their gazes connected, and the corner of his mouth hitched. "I never figured I'd have this problem with you. You're not my type."

Oh, he was so her type, though. Caroline obviously didn't voice that. Besides, she'd had nothing but rotten luck with her type. It was time to try something…

She couldn't immediately fill in the blank. *Boring* finally came to mind. But maybe boring was exactly what she needed.

Too bad it wasn't what she wanted.

What she wanted was Egan.

The wine was going straight to her head, and the need was going straight through her body.

"What *is* your type?" she asked. She was playing with fire, and she was so close that she took in his scent. No aftershave today. Because he hadn't shaved. He smelled like clean cotton from his shirt, leather from his boots and the rest was all just the scent of a man.

He opened his mouth. Closed it. Shook his head. "You don't really want to know."

"But I do. What's your type?" she repeated, touching the rim of her wine glass to his chest.

Something dark and dangerous went through his eyes. "My type is someone temporary."

"Temporary," she repeated. She felt another sting and set her glass on the counter. "As in love 'em and leave 'em?"

"I don't love them. I've never said that to anyone I was involved with, and I've never implied it."

Her mouth dropped open. "You've never said I love you?"

"Never. I have fun with them, period. And they know that's all it's going to be right from the start." Egan mumbled a four-letter word. "That's my type, Caroline, and that's why you should back away."

So, she was dealing with a man who'd never said I love you. A man, from the sound of it, who'd never had a serious relationship. Why didn't that make her listen to him and back away?

Because she was obviously as warped as he was.

Caroline couldn't help herself. She wanted to put a dent in that rugged facade, although she wasn't entirely sure it was a facade. That was part of the lure. The uncertainty of what he would do.

The lack of boredom.

The attraction so strong that it could consume her.

She leaned in—to do what, Caroline didn't know. She just wanted to get closer to see how he'd react.

He reacted all right.

Egan latched on to her wrists, and in the same motion, he whirled around and put her back against the door frame. He wasn't exactly gentle. And his eyes burned with a fire that Caroline understood all too well.

He moved closer all right, until his mouth was almost touching hers. Until his body was closer, too. Until his shirt brushed against her breasts. Now *that* sent a nice shiver through her.

She wanted him to touch her. And she wanted it more than her next breath. But he didn't touch. Instead, that fiery blue gaze went from her hair. To her eyes. To her cheeks. To her mouth.

Caressing her.

And he was doing it in a way she'd never thought of as intimate. Leave it to Egan to make air kisses as potent as the real thing.

"You don't want a piece of me," Egan warned.

But it sounded like an invitation to her aroused body. An invitation she couldn't accept. She reminded herself of what Egan had said about losing focus. Oh, yes. This was the ultimate losing-focus activity. Air kissing and with her body so ready that she was imagining sex on the kitchen island.

Caroline couldn't make the desire go away.

Egan apparently didn't have that problem.

He let go of her as if she'd scalded him, and using his forearm, he eased her aside. He no longer had those baby blues on her lips. He was looking at the underside of the cabinet next to them.

"Did you know that was there?" he mouthed.

Expecting to see a brown scorpion or some other unsavory critter, Caroline followed his pointing index finger. It took her a moment to spot what had grabbed his attention, but she finally saw the "thing" stuck to the bottom of the cabinet. It was black, round and about the size of a quarter.

"What is it?" she asked. God, please don't let it be another bomb, but it looked too small for that.

Egan motioned for her to stay quiet. He moved her away from it and into the living room. By the time they made those few steps, she was more than a little concerned. Her heart was racing. So were her thoughts. And these weren't good thoughts, either.

"Did you know it was there?" he asked, putting his mouth directly against her ear.

"No. What is it?"

"An eavesdropping device. Caroline, someone's listening to us."

Chapter Eight

Hell.

And Egan silently repeated that profanity multiple times when the full realization about the eavesdropping device hit him.

Someone had likely overheard Caroline's entire drug-induced session with the psychiatrist. That someone could have also heard Caroline's and his conversations. Both the personal ones and the ones involving the case. And that meant this someone would know she was recovering bits and pieces of her lost memories.

Critical memories that could identify a killer.

"What do we do?" Caroline whispered. Because he was so close to her, he could feel her arm trembling.

"Play along," he whispered back. "I think I'll get started on some of that paperwork," Egan then said louder. "Go ahead and finish your sandwich and save me some Oreos."

It was, hopefully, a casual-sounding comment that Egan wanted the listener to overhear so the person would think all was normal. He didn't want to set off alarms just yet in case it was possible to trace where the device was transmitting.

A killer could be on the receiving end.

Egan motioned for Caroline to follow him, and he led her through the kitchen. He used a dish towel from one of the drawers to muffle the little beeps that sounded as he disengaged the security system. And he eased open the door that led to the back porch.

It was dark already, and there wasn't much of a moon because of the cloudy sky. He didn't turn on the lights, but there was more than enough illumination from the lagoon-colored pool. Egan maneuvered her away from that area and to the corner of the porch. There was still too much light to make him feel secure with having her outside, so he took her to the side of the house and pulled her behind a row of mountain laurels where they were in the shadows.

The ground was wet and soggy, not just from the recent rain but from Caroline's automatic sprinkler system that had obviously come on. He could hear the spraying water on the other side of the house. Maybe the sprinkler and the pool filtering system would drown out what they said. While he was hoping, he added that maybe the range of the eavesdropping device wouldn't extend to the yard.

"There could be other devices inside," he explained. "It's not safe to talk in there."

Caroline gave a choppy nod and looked exactly as he expected her to look. As if she'd been delivered another blow. Which she had.

Egan took out his cell phone and called Hayes at the Cantara Hill Country Club. "We have another problem," Egan started. He kept his voice low just in case. "There's a listening device in Caroline's kitchen."

"You're kidding?" Hayes grumbled.

"I wish."

"Well, this just keeps getting more and more complicated."

Yes. And Egan didn't like this particular complication.
"How fast can you get equipment up here to check it out?
I want to find the source of reception."

"Yeah. I'd like to know that, too," Hayes agreed. "I
don't have any equipment like that here with me, but the
San Antonio office will. I'll call them and have someone
bring it over right away. It might take a half hour or so,
but just hang tight, I'll get there."

"Thanks." Egan clicked End Call and put his phone
back in his pocket.

"Who's doing this to me?" Caroline whispered.

"I don't know." But they knew it was probably the
killer. Or someone working for the killer. "I don't know
how long that device has been there, but I couldn't see
any dust on it. Did anyone recently have access to your
house when you weren't here?"

She took a moment, obviously thinking. "I have a
housekeeper who comes in twice a week. She doesn't
even have a key because my mother lets her in. The
woman cleans both our houses, and I don't suspect her."

Neither did Egan, but he'd still check her out. It was a
long shot, though, because it wouldn't have taken much
time to plant that bug. Mere seconds. Which led him to
his next question. "Has Kenneth been inside the house
since we started the investigation?"

Caroline shook her head. "No. Wait, yes. Tammy and
he were here with my parents the night Vincent
Montoya's body was discovered."

"Of course they were." Now, that didn't surprise

Egan, and it was the reason Kenneth was still his number one suspect.

"What if the intruder is the one who put the device there?" Caroline asked.

Unfortunately, Egan couldn't rule that out. "If we go with the possibility that the intruder didn't set the bomb, that he didn't try to kill you two nights ago, then he could have planted the listening device. Maybe in addition to the dream journal, he wanted to hear what you were saying. Maybe he was listening for any clues as to what you knew. Clues that could ultimately incriminate him."

She hesitated, then nodded. "That means we're back to my memory issues."

"But the question is—what would a killer think you could remember that would point the finger at him?"

Caroline lifted her shoulder as if the answer were obvious. "Something to do with the hit-and-run."

"Maybe." Egan played around with that in his mind. "And maybe it's connected to that conversation you had with Kimberly the night she died. The secret affair she mentioned and the argument Kimberly had with Kenneth."

"You think her secret lover could be behind this?"

Egan opened his mouth to say yes, it was entirely possible, but he didn't have time to respond. That's because he heard the snap. That was it. Just a snippet of a sound that made him reach for his gun.

But it was already too late.

Someone fired a shot.

CAROLINE'S HEART JUMPED to her throat.

She heard the sound. Not loud. More like a swish. In

itself, it wasn't enough to be alarming, but it was Egan's reaction that made her realize what was happening.

That swishing sound was a bullet being fired.

Egan drew his firearm and pushed her to the muddy ground, behind the flowering lantana and sage that grew beneath the mountain laurels. He didn't stop there. He got in front of her. Protecting her.

He jerked out his phone again and pressed a button on it. Probably to redial Hayes. Thankfully, he wasn't far away, and if he responded immediately, he should be there in just a couple of minutes.

She prayed that would be soon enough.

"Someone's shooting at us," Egan said softly. "We're on the west side of Caroline's house."

Another shot.

This one whistled through the darkness and landed mere inches from her feet. She drew up her legs, trying to leave as little of herself exposed as possible. But that wouldn't do anything to help Egan. He was there. Right in front of her. Where he could easily be killed.

Oh, God.

Why was this happening?

The bomb had been one thing. Sinister, yes. But she hadn't even known it was there. If it'd gone off with her in the car, she literally wouldn't have known what had hit her. But this…she knew these bullets were being aimed at her.

Egan lifted his gun. Aimed at a thick live oak that was just on the other side of the wrought-iron fence in Taylor's yard. He fired. That sound wasn't a swish or soft whistle. It was a blast that nearly deafened her.

Caroline covered her ears with her hands, but it was too little too late. Egan fired again.

So did the shooter.

Not just one bullet, either. But the gunman fired three shots in rapid succession. Egan had no choice but to drop down, taking himself out of position to return fire. But hopefully, this new position would save his life.

The next shot went to the right of their heads. It was too close. And it shattered the limestone flanking at the base of the house and sent shards flying through the air. Caroline felt one of those sharp pieces slice across her cheek, but she didn't react. She stayed quiet. Because any noise might give away their exact position. Right now, that was all they could do to keep from being killed because they were literally pinned down with no place to run.

"Stay low and don't move," Egan whispered.

Caroline wished that he would do the same thing, and she nearly latched on to him and dragged him back when he levered himself up and returned fire. She couldn't tell where his shots had landed, but they seemed to go in the direction of that live oak.

Was the shooter perched in that tree?

If so, the person must have cut through Taylor's yard. So did that mean it truly was someone she knew? Someone familiar with the landscape and points of access to her property? Of course, it wouldn't be that difficult for an intruder to sneak through the darkness, climb the tree and deliver those shots.

But how had the gunman known that Egan and she would be outside?

Damn.

Maybe the intruder had used the eavesdropping device. Or were there possibly other devices planted outside? Or worse—did the intruder have them under actual surveillance?

Caroline wanted to curse and scream. When would this dangerous invasion of her life end? And when was that danger going to stop extending to people around her? The danger was especially high for Egan, who was literally in the line of fire. With each of those bullets, he'd endangered his own life while saving hers.

Another bullet smacked into the mountain laurel overhead, and the shattered branches rained down on them. Egan immediately returned fire, sending two bullets in the direction of the shooter.

Caroline heard sirens in the distance. Probably Hayes. Thank God. Egan needed the backup, and if they got lucky, the sirens might stop the shooter.

Or not.

The thought had barely formed in her head when there was another shot. Then another. And another. Until Caroline lost count.

Egan dropped back down to cover, and they waited there. Long, agonizing moments. For what seemed an eternity. Until the frantic rounds of gunfire stopped.

Just like that.

The sirens got louder and closer, and so did the sound of the approaching vehicle. From what she could tell, the driver braked to a screeching halt at the end of her driveway.

"Egan?" Hayes yelled.

"Over here. Use the nightscope to check the big tree in Taylor's yard."

Silence followed. It was both a good and bad sound. There were no more shots fired, but the silence meant the shooter was likely getting away.

"We can't move yet," Egan explained to her. "This could be a trick to draw us out."

She hadn't thought of that. And here she was just beginning to think that this latest attempt to kill her would soon be over.

It might have just begun.

"I don't see anything," Hayes shouted. "But I'll have a closer look. Stay put."

Caroline wasn't sure she could move anyway. So she lay there on the wet ground next to Egan. With the adrenaline pulsing through her and her heart beating so hard that she thought it might crack her ribs, it was hard to imagine that her life would ever get back to normal.

"I'm sorry this happened," Egan said to her.

"Yes. I'm sorry, too."

Even with all the precautions they'd taken, they hadn't been able to prevent the attack.

She heard another vehicle come to a stop in her driveway and then heard Hayes call out to them. It was the private security guards, obviously coming as additional backup.

"Nothing," Hayes relayed.

That single word caused Egan to curse. And Caroline knew why. It meant the gunman had gotten away again. They weren't safe, and they wouldn't be until this guy was caught.

Egan stood and pulled her to her feet. Thank goodness he kept his arm around her waist because her legs were wobbly, and she wasn't sure she could stand on her own.

Hayes walked toward them. "I'll take a look around the area."

Egan nodded. "I think the shooter used a rifle rigged with a silencer. He wasn't close enough to use a handgun."

"Obviously this wasn't a pro, or we wouldn't be standing here talking," Hayes concluded.

If there was a silver lining in this, there it was. The irony of this crazy situation. The gunman hadn't been a professional assassin but more likely a friend or a neighbor.

Hayes tipped his head to Caroline. "You might want to go ahead and get her out of here."

Egan looked at her first, and he must have seen the shock and the fear that was still no doubt on her face. "I'll take her to the office at the country club." He turned to the guards. "I want all gates to Cantara Hills closed and locked. No one gets in or out."

Probably because he'd barked that order and had fire in his eyes, the guard issued a "yes, sir" and got moving.

Egan turned back to Hayes. "As soon as you've checked out that tree, start rounding up everyone in the entire neighborhood. Everyone is going to be tested for gunshot residue."

Hayes's eyebrow lifted. "Everyone?"

"*Everyone,*" Egan confirmed through clenched teeth.

Chapter Nine

Egan wasn't mad. He was a dozen steps past that particular emotion.

And along with being past mad, he was plenty tired of hearing rich people complain about having to be tested for gunshot residue. He didn't care a lick about the inconvenience to them or about their feelings.

He had one goal.

Find the shooter.

He wanted to deal personally with the SOB who'd nearly killed Caroline.

Egan glanced at her to see how she was holding up. She was seated in the corner of his office, sipping a cup of reheated coffee. She'd changed into his shirt because hers had been coated with mud, and she'd washed up. But water and a clean shirt couldn't erase the worry he saw on her face.

He wished he could get her away from all of this, but he couldn't. Brody's flight still hadn't landed, and he needed to assist with the GSR testing. Besides, Egan wanted to be there if and when they identified the culprit.

Kenneth Sutton and his wife, Tammy, were the next to

be tested. When they walked through the door of the office, both glared furiously at Egan, and expressed their extreme displeasure at being called into the temporary office and treated like criminals.

Hayes used the surface of the desk to hold the supplies for the procedure, which involved four nitric acid swabs per person—swabs for the fronts of their hands and the backs. That way, if there was any GSR present, they would detect it.

The security guards were in the adjacent office, testing some of the residents. Along with them was a CSI that SAPD had sent over. With luck, they wouldn't have to swab everyone before they got a match.

"She's clean," Hayes announced when he swabbed Tammy's hands.

"I told you," she grumbled. She folded her arms over her ample chest and waited while Hayes repeated the procedure on her husband.

Egan stepped closer. He didn't want to miss this. Because if he had to put money on who had fired those shots, his money would be on Kenneth.

Hayes did the first swab and drew it back. Clean. Egan's stomach sank a little. He really wanted to nail this guy. But Hayes produced another clean swab.

"I'm innocent," Kenneth declared. "I appreciate that you want to find this person. I want to find him, too. But it's not me. Nor my wife."

The third swab was negative, too.

Kenneth locked his gaze with Egan's just as Hayes declared the fourth swab to be clean.

Kenneth stood and looked at Caroline. "Is there anything I can do for you? Anything you need?"

Caroline shook her head and seemed totally unconvinced about the man's concern. That's probably because Egan had already alerted her that Kenneth, Tammy or any of the other residents could have showered and changed their clothes after the shooting. That could be the reason there was no gunshot residue on their hands. In other words, Kenneth and/or his wife could still be guilty as sin.

Kenneth and Tammy stormed out, and Hayes motioned for the next person to enter the room. It was his father, Walt.

Walt didn't acknowledge him. Looking completely at ease, he strolled into the room. Of course, his father was likely familiar and even comfortable with every inch of the country club as well as the rest of Cantara Hills since he'd worked for Link Hathaway for nearly thirty-five years, five years before Egan had even been born.

Hayes started the swabs on Walt while Egan tested the next resident, a young woman who lived in the Cantara Hills condos.

"You do know you're riling a lot of people," Walt said, his voice practically a whisper.

Much to Egan's disgust, he couldn't ignore his father's warning. Not because his father had given him many warnings when he was growing up. But because Walt almost never interacted with him unless he was extremely upset—like the time Egan had beaten up Carlson Woodward.

"Yeah, I get accused of riling people a lot," Egan commented.

That's when Walt looked at Egan. A surprise, since he wasn't big on eye contact, either. "Be careful not to rile the wrong people," his father mumbled.

Egan stared back at him. "That sounds like a threat."

No confirmation of that. When the four swabs showed negative results, Walt stood and calmly walked out.

However, there was nothing calm about the way Egan felt. He cursed his reaction and wondered how many lifetimes it would take him to become immune to the cold disinterest of the man who'd fathered him.

Egan dismissed the woman he tested after her swabs were all negative, and he motioned for the next person to enter. It was Miles Landis, and he had that smirky grin on his face. A smirk he aimed at Caroline. That's when Egan knew that Caroline couldn't be subjected to this all night. He went to her and helped her stand.

"Come with me," Egan instructed.

He led her to the back of the room where there was a door to his adjoining suite, the place he'd been staying since the investigation. Egan opened the door and ushered her inside. "Why don't you take a shower and get some rest."

"Right," she said, both of them knowing that rest wouldn't come. "I want to know who's responsible."

"I want to know that, too, but having you out there won't make it happen any sooner." He heard the anger in his voice and knew it shouldn't be aimed at her. "You'll be safe here. The other entrance is blocked off. I'll make sure no one gets in."

She nodded. And stood there. Staring at him. "Thank you for saving my life, again."

"You shouldn't be thanking me. When I took you outside, I nearly let you get killed."

"You nearly got yourself killed." She pulled in a long breath.

Man—Egan wanted to hold her, to assure her that he would make things right. But he couldn't. Because he wasn't certain he could fix things. And one hug wouldn't be enough. Not with the adrenaline churning through both of them.

He settled for skimming his finger over her cheek. "I'll help Hayes with the testing. The sooner we swab everyone, the sooner we'll know who fired those shots."

She nodded. "Tell me the second you find something."

"I will," he promised.

Egan went back into the office and could deduce from Miles's continuing smirk that he hadn't tested positive. Still, there was something that Egan wanted to ask the man.

He motioned for Miles to go to the corner of the room. "I didn't fire those shots," Miles volunteered. "I don't have a reason to hurt Caroline."

Egan didn't even address that. "How well did you know Kimberly McQuade, the woman killed in the hit-and-run?"

Miles looked more than a little surprised. "I knew her. Why?"

"Any idea if there was a man in her life?"

"You mean a lover." Miles didn't wait for confirmation, and he appeared to give that some thought. "I never saw her with anyone, but I know that Trent Briggs wanted to get in her pants."

Briggs, Kenneth's aide, one of the murder victims. During the investigation, Egan had heard rumors that Trent had unsuccessfully pursued Kimberly, but if he'd succeeded, there would have been no reason for Kimberly to keep an affair secret.

"How about Kenneth?" Egan asked. "Any idea if he wanted to get in her pants, too?"

The smirk returned. "Kenneth? Not a chance." Miles

glanced back at the line of people waiting to be tested. "But you'll want to ask our tennis pro about that."

"Carlson Woodward?" The bucket of slime who'd made his childhood a living hell? "Why do I want to ask him?"

Miles leaned in and lowered his voice. "Figure it out." And with that ominous comment, he sauntered away.

"Next," Hayes called out.

Egan heard the guards in the other office call out the same. At the speed they were going and with five of them doing the processing, it might not take all night. Of course, he'd have to do a follow-up to make sure everyone had been tested because it was entirely likely that the shooter might try to evade this whole process.

But the one person who had his attention now was Carlson. It boiled Egan's blood to think this man might have had something to do with anyone Egan knew.

Link Hathaway entered, and he wasn't alone. His daughter, Margaret, was with him, and Egan could see his father still in the makeshift waiting area. Walt had probably driven the two of them there and would drive them back home.

As expected, Link complained, cursed and threatened to sue them while Egan swabbed his hands, but that wasn't what caught Egan's attention.

It was Margaret.

She trembled as Hayes processed her. Her behavior was enough to alarm Egan, but he relaxed when she tested negative.

Her father didn't test positive, either.

Finally, it was Carlson Woodward's turn. Tall, dark and slimy. He still wore his tennis clothes, and his hair was damp. Perhaps he'd been giving a lesson. He didn't have

Miles's smirk. No, he was in a public place. Egan knew firsthand that Carlson saved his smirks and taunts for times when he didn't feel the need to impress anyone.

Egan caught his arm and pulled him to the other side of the room. "Talk to me about Kimberly McQuade."

Carlson stared at Egan's grip and waited until he let go of him before he answered. "She's dead," Carlson said under his breath. He glanced behind him, probably to see who might overhear this conversation.

"Did you try to start something with her?" Egan asked.

He studied Egan a moment. "Define *something*."

Egan debated how much he should say and finally decided to put it all out there. "An affair."

Carlson's eyes lit up as if he'd just been handed a delicious morsel to savor. Egan didn't like being the one who gave him that morsel, but he had to question people about this affair because it could provide him with information about the identity of the killer.

Egan thought of Caroline. Of the shock and fear he'd seen on her face. And he knew he had to do whatever it took to get answers. He couldn't continue to risk her life.

"You think I slept with your Ranger buddy's sister?" Carlson clarified. He grinned.

It took every bit of Egan's willpower not to punch that grin right off his face. "Just answer the question."

Still grinning, Carlson leaned in and put his mouth close to Egan's ear. "She came on to me, but I turned her down. I don't sleep with the trash. That's the exact reason I turned down Caroline. She might be rich, but that doesn't change the kind of woman she is. Trash is trash, no matter how big the trust fund."

Egan didn't bother with willpower. He shoved Carlson

against the wall, and that had Hayes barreling across the room. "What's going on here?"

"I'm just telling the truth," Carlson gleefully explained. Oh, he was enjoying this, and Egan instantly regretted the burst of temper. Carlson fed on that kind of crap.

Hayes gave each of them a long, hard look before he latched on to Carlson and pulled him back to the desk. "Hold out your hands," Hayes ordered.

Egan didn't assist him, mainly because he'd end up breaking every one of Carlson's fingers.

Hayes stiffened, and Egan went closer to see what had caused his fellow Ranger's reaction.

And there it was.

The swabs had turned blue.

An indication that gunshot residue was present. This was no small amount, either. The entire swabs had lit up.

Egan stared at Carlson, almost hoping the man would go for a gun or try to escape. "Well?"

No gun and no escape. Carlson grinned again. "Oh, did I forget to tell you that I was at the firing range this afternoon? With all the crime in Cantara Hills, I thought I should learn how to defend myself." He shook his head. "You just can't get good law enforcement help these days."

Egan stepped closer, but Hayes stood, blocking him. Which was probably a good thing. Best not to beat the hell out of a suspect.

And Carlson was now, indeed, a suspect.

"What's the name of the firing range?" Hayes asked.

"Millford Crest. It's about fifteen minutes from here. My instructor is Jerry Bradshaw. He gives lessons to lots of people from Cantara Hills."

The Reader Service — Here's how it works:

Accepting your 2 free books and 2 free mystery gifts places you under no obligation to buy anything. You may keep the books and gifts and return the shipping statement marked "cancel". If you do not cancel, about a month later we'll send you 6 additional books and bill you just $4.24 each in the U.S. or $4.99 each in Canada, plus 25¢ shipping & handling per book and applicable taxes if any.* That's the complete price and at a savings of at least 15% off the cover price, it's quite a bargain! You may cancel at any time, but if you choose to continue, every month we'll send you 6 more books which you may either purchase at the discount price or return to us and cancel your subscription.

*Terms and prices subject to change without notice. Sales tax applicable in N.Y. Canadian residents will be charged applicable provincial taxes and GST. Offer not valid in Quebec. Credit or debit balances in a customer's account(s) may be offset by any other outstanding balance owed by or to the customer. Please allow 4 to 6 weeks for delivery. Offer available while quantities last.

If offer card is missing write to: The Harlequin Reader Service, 3010 Walden Ave., P.O. Box 1867, Buffalo NY 14240-1867

NO POSTAGE
NECESSARY
IF MAILED
IN THE
UNITED STATES

BUSINESS REPLY MAIL

FIRST-CLASS MAIL   PERMIT NO. 717   BUFFALO, NY

POSTAGE WILL BE PAID BY ADDRESSEE

HARLEQUIN READER SERVICE
3010 WALDEN AVE
PO BOX 1867
BUFFALO NY 14240-9952

Play the
Lucky
Hearts
Game

and get...

2 FREE BOOKS and
2 FREE MYSTERY GIFTS...

yes! YOURS to KEEP!

I have scratched off the silver card.
Please send me my *2 FREE BOOKS* and *2 FREE*
mystery GIFTS (gifts are worth about $10). I
understand that I am under no obligation to purchase
any books as explained on the back of this card.

Scratch Here!

then look below to see
what your cards get you...
2 Free Books & 2 Free
Mystery Gifts!

382 HDL ESSX   ## 182 HDL ESWA

FIRST NAME	LAST NAME

ADDRESS

APT.#	CITY

STATE/PROV.	ZIP/POSTAL CODE

(H-I-07/08)

Twenty-one gets you
2 FREE BOOKS and
2 FREE MYSTERY GIFTS!

Twenty gets you
2 FREE BOOKS!

Nineteen gets you
1 FREE BOOK!

TRY AGAIN!

▲ DETACH AND MAIL CARD TODAY! ▲

Hayes jotted down the information. "This Bradshaw will verify you were there today?"

"Of course."

Hayes grabbed the phone and used 4-1-1 to get the number of the firing range. While he was busy with that, Egan continued the questioning. "Where were you at eight-fifteen tonight?"

He shrugged. "Well, I wasn't shooting at you, Sgt. Caldwell."

Egan leaned in, violating his personal space. "Where. Were. You. Tonight?" He overly enunciated each word.

"Here, at my office at the country club. Besides, what possible motive would I have for wanting you dead?"

"Bad blood," Egan readily answered. People had killed for less. "If what you say is true, if you were really in your office tonight, then that'll be on the surveillance cameras." He hoped.

"Oh, that might be a problem," Carlson volunteered. He made a show of looking disappointed. "The one outside my office has been broken for days. I reported it, I think."

"Yeah, I'll bet you did."

Egan was more than ready to arrest this sorry excuse for a human being, but he heard Hayes say something that he didn't want to hear.

"The firing range instructor confirmed that Carlson was there," Hayes relayed. "Don't worry. After Brody arrives, I'll go out and have a chat with this guy and see if there are any holes in his story."

If that concerned Carlson in the least, he didn't show it. In fact, he seemed to enjoy it. Was he playing some kind of deadly game of cat and mouse? Because he could have intentionally gone to the firing range just to cover up the premeditated attack on Caroline and him.

Egan quickly worked through how that info fit the rest of the murders. Maybe Carlson was the one who'd hired Montoya to cause that hit-and-run so he could get back at Brody. There was bad blood from childhood between Carlson and Brody. And all the other killings and attempts could have resulted from that.

Carlson had just moved to the top of his list of suspects.

"Am I free to go?" Carlson asked.

It truly pained Egan to say this. "For now. But don't go far."

"Wouldn't dream of it. Cantara Hills is my home away from home." He looked around the office, and his gaze landed on the door to the suite. Where Caroline was. "In fact, I know every room in this entire club."

It sounded like a threat. A bad one. And Egan had to force himself not to bolt to go check on Caroline. He waited until Carlson had issued a smug "See you later" before he took Hayes aside.

"I don't think it's a good idea for Caroline to be in that room alone," Egan explained.

Hayes nodded. "I can make sure the rest of the swabs get done. Don't worry about it."

But Egan was worrying. And he was thinking. About what Caroline was no doubt feeling. She needed someone, a shoulder to cry on, and he was tired of pushing her away.

"Officially, I want Caroline in your protective custody," Egan insisted. "I want that in the paperwork, and I'll add it when I do my report about the shooting."

Hayes flexed his eyebrows. "Does that mean you want me to stay with her tonight?"

"No." And Egan was fully aware of how that sounded. "But I'd like you to stay put out here, to make sure no one tries to get inside."

"Right." Hayes paused. Then, paused some more. "I've seen the way you look at Caroline. You think being with her is wise?"

"No." It was probably the biggest mistake he'd ever make. But knowing that wouldn't stop him.

Chapter Ten

Caroline nearly jumped out of her skin when she heard the doorknob turn. Every inch of her was on edge, and she couldn't stop reliving the terrifying images of lying in that mud while someone had tried to murder Egan and her.

She waited, with her hand flattened against her chest, and she watched as the door opened.

Egan walked in.

Relief flooded through her. Well, as much relief as she could feel after everything that had happened. Egan obviously felt the same. She could see the tension in his face and shoulders.

"What's wrong?" she asked.

"Maybe nothing." But it didn't sound that way. It sounded like something big. "Carlson Woodward tested positive for gunshot residue."

Of all the people she'd thought who might test positive, he wasn't one of them. "He's the shooter?"

Egan shrugged. "He was at a firing range earlier in the day. That could account for it."

He didn't add the obvious—that the other explanation was that not only had Carlson been at the firing range but he had also tried to kill them.

But had Carlson really done that?

It seemed extreme. Unless he was linked to Vincent Montoya and those other murders. Or maybe the child-hood grudge between Egan and him was a lot more than just a grudge.

Egan locked the door, using the deadbolt and the chain, and he walked closer, studying her clothes. She was wearing one of his blue work shirts and a pair of his boxers.

"This is all I could find," she explained. Maybe if she concentrated on conversation or anything else other than the shooting, those images would go away. "You really don't own any pajamas, do you?"

He stopped just inches away from her. The corner of his mouth lifted. A half smile. But the smile didn't make it all the way to his eyes. "I'll see if Taylor can bring you something to wear."

"She's not home tonight. I already called her. She's on a business trip for her charity foundation and won't be back until tomorrow morning." Caroline wanted to keep talking. She wanted to keep thinking about clothes, about Taylor, about anything that would keep her mind occupied.

She refused to cry, but she felt the tears building. And the fear. *Mercy,* when was that going to pass?

"You're no longer in my protective custody," Egan said. It sounded like an announcement.

And it apparently was.

Because he immediately pulled her into his arms.

That embrace was more than warm strength and comfort. It was necessary. And she needed it. Just like that, Caroline shattered. She couldn't fight it any longer. The tears came, and she fell apart.

Egan was right there to make sure she didn't fall too hard.

"I don't usually cry," she heard herself say.

"It wasn't a usual night."

She didn't accept that as an excuse. "But you're not a basket case."

Egan leaned back a little and looked down at her. "Yes, I am."

Their eyes met, and she saw it then. Not just the tension. But the uneasiness that ran bone-deep inside him. This shooting had been a nightmare and had brought them together like nothing else could have.

They'd cheated death, together.

He understood everything she was going through, and she instinctively knew that no one but Egan would be able to comfort her. Or maybe it was simply that she didn't want anyone else to.

Caroline stood there, blinking back the tears. Egan wiped the ones that fell from her cheeks, and in the same motion, his mouth came to hers.

She was stunned. But for only a second. Her mind barely had time to process the surprise before she felt the other sensation. Pleasure. It wasn't just his embrace that she needed. She needed this, too, and Egan gave it to her.

His mouth moved over hers. He wasn't rough, but he wasn't gentle. He took her, sliding his hand behind her neck so that he controlled the movement of her head.

Caroline didn't care about the loss of control. She allowed the searing heat from that kiss to fire through her, and she took everything Egan was offering.

She wrapped her arms around him. No gentle motion from her, either. That kiss had sparked a torrent of feelings that immediately became an avalanche. Caroline pulled him closer, until their bodies were pressed against each other, breath against skin, and she returned the kiss.

Egan did indeed taste as good as he looked.

She'd felt passion before. Had even been on the receiving end of some good kisses. But this went up several levels. And in the back of her mind, Caroline realized this kiss, this moment, would become the benchmark she would to use to measure all others.

That wasn't exactly a comforting thought.

Still, it didn't stop her. Nothing would at this point. She wanted to feel. She wanted the heat.

She wanted Egan.

His grip tightened around the back of her neck. The kiss deepened, and his tongue touched hers. More fire. More need. She fought to get closer.

Egan kept control. Well, at least until she slid her hand between their bodies and touched the front of his jeans. He made one rough sound. A hitch in breath that was muffled by the kiss, and then he backed her up against the wall. Using just one of his hands, he cupped her wrists and pinned them in place over her head.

They were going to have sex.

That was the only conclusion Caroline could see happening from this. The emotions were too high. The heat too intense.

And he was such a good kisser.

He didn't stop with just kissing her mouth. He went to her neck and started some major fires there as well. Caroline was aware of that heated sensation in that particular part of her body, but it was competing with all the other sensations. Especially those caused by his hand, as it slid down to cup her right breast.

Egan swiped his thumb over her nipple.

Then, he unbuttoned her shirt and replaced his thumb with his mouth.

Oh, mercy.

That nipple kiss made her want to beg for more, but it was mild compared to what happened when his mouth returned to hers. He adjusted their positions, until his hard sex touched hers. His boxers that she was wearing weren't much of a barrier. Hardly anything at all.

And she felt every inch of him.

She wanted him inside her right then. Just anticipating it nearly made her climax.

Caroline fought to free her hands so she could go after his zipper. But Egan just held on and slid them both to the floor. With her back still against the wall, she landed with her knees cradling his hips. It wasn't quite enough contact, so she maneuvered her hips closer so she could rub against his erection.

It was an overwhelming sensation.

But soon, it wasn't enough.

Egan seemed to know the exact moment when she had to have more.

Now, Caroline said to herself. Finally, it was going to happen. They were going to have wild, hot, crazy, rough sex.

But he still didn't let her go after his zipper.

Caroline groaned in protest, but the groan died on her lips when he gave their bodies another adjustment. He turned, laying her on the floor, and he finally released her hands. *Yes!* However, the zipper thing didn't happen.

Because he turned the tables on her.

Before Caroline even knew his intent, the boxer shorts

came off her. She felt the chill of the A/C on the inside of her thighs. For only a second. Then, she felt Egan's warmth.

And Egan's mouth.

Now, this was a French kiss to remember.

He literally made love to her with his mouth. Caroline considered, briefly, a protest. She considered telling him that she wanted him inside her. She wanted them to find release together, but after a flick of tongue and the not-so-gentle coaxing of his mouth, she gave up and slid her fingers into his hair.

She lifted her hips, moving with his kiss. He was so good at this. Not a surprise. And it didn't surprise her that within seconds, he had her close to that edge. Caroline wanted to savor it, to savor him, longer. But Egan would have no part of that. He continued to do what he was doing until she felt her body do the only thing it could.

Surrender.

The climax racked through her. It was as hard and as intense as the man responsible for what she was feeling.

She couldn't move right away. The aftershocks continued to ripple through her. Her heart reacted by racing like crazy. And her breathing was labored. But all those bodily reactions didn't make her forget the aroused man between her legs.

Caroline reached for him, but like before, he caught on to her hands and shook his head.

She couldn't believe that head shake. "No fair," she insisted.

"It's fair." He made his way back up her body and kissed her.

She tried not to let that kiss distract her, either. "How do you figure that? I got all the pleasure. You did all the work."

"That wasn't work." Egan freed her hands, rolled away from her and sat up, propping himself against the wall. "Feel better?"

"Oh." It took her a moment to process that. She didn't process it well. "That was to make me feel better?"

"No. It was to make *me* feel better. But I was hoping it'd do the same to you."

Caroline didn't know whether he was lying or not. Or whether to be insulted. She wasn't into sympathy orgasms, though secretly she had to admit that a sympathy orgasm from Egan was better than a regular one. Still...

"Caroline," he said, looking down at her.

Uh-oh. She knew that look and that tone. She was about to get a talk about how this couldn't mean anything. He'd probably remind her of the case, and the danger.

She pulled up her boxers, sat up and met him eye-to-eye. Best to nip this in the bud.

"I feel better," she announced. Caroline held out her hand to prove that she was no longer trembling—thank goodness, she wasn't—and just in case Egan hadn't gotten the point, she hiked up her chin. "You're better than a prescription sedative. So, consider your job done for the night, Sgt. Caldwell."

His "look" changed, and something primal and dangerous went through his scorching blue eyes. She'd pushed him too far.

Good!

Caroline wanted to push him farther.

She wanted to see if she could put a crack in that cool, imperturbable composure. Part of her, the obviously aroused, insane part of her, wanted to know what it would feel like to cause Egan to take her completely.

But he didn't take her, completely or otherwise.

He calmly got up, without saying a word, and disappeared into the bathroom, leaving her there with a lot of questions about what the heck had just happened.

They had an insane so-called relationship going on here. Oral sex and anger. Anger because Egan Caldwell thought it was perfectly all right to give her the orgasm of her life without allowing her the opportunity to do the same to him. This was his way of keeping his distance. That love 'em and leave 'em garbage. Or rather that have sex and leave 'em philosophy that he'd lived by.

Caroline was still in the middle of her mental tirade when there was a knock at the door. She froze. Egan didn't. He must have heard the sound because he came rocketing out of the bathroom, and before he reached the door, he already had his gun drawn.

"Sgt. Caldwell?" someone said from the other side. Caroline recognized it as the voice of one of the civilian security guards. "You have a visitor."

"Who is it?" Egan didn't put his gun away, and he certainly didn't sound welcoming.

"Carlson Woodward. He's the tennis pro here, and he says he needs to speak to you, that it's important."

"Go into the bathroom," Egan instructed Caroline.

She considered refusing because if Carlson was indeed guilty, she wanted to face him down. But Egan would never allow that. To save them both an argument, she stepped into the adjoining bathroom, but Caroline left the door ajar so she could see and hear everything.

Egan waited until she was in place before he opened the main door. The guard was there, and behind him was Carlson.

"We finished the swabs," the guard explained. "Mr. Woodward here is the only one who tested positive. He left and then came back because he said he had to talk to you. I searched him. He's not carrying a weapon."

Egan peered out into the office. "Where's Hayes?"

"With the club manager, Michael DeCalley. They're checking the surveillance camera outside Mr. Woodward's office. They're just around the corner and said they'd be back in a couple of minutes. The other Ranger should be here shortly, too. Lt. McQuade called, and he's on his way from the airport now."

Good. Caroline wanted Hayes and Brody there for backup, just in case.

Carlson stepped forward, moving to the guard's side. "I didn't come armed. I'm merely here with information."

"About what?" Egan snapped. The guard dropped back, walking in the direction of the desk, where they'd done the GSR testing.

But Carlson didn't answer. He looked past Egan, and his gaze landed right on her. His eyes immediately lit up, and Caroline didn't have to guess why. She no doubt looked as if she'd just gotten off the floor with Egan.

"Well, well, Caroline Stallings," Carlson said. He grinned from ear to ear. "How do you think your parents are going to take the news when they hear you're bedding down deep with the likes of a lowly Texas Ranger? A chauffeur's son, at that."

She did not need this.

Egan latched on to a handful of Carlson's shirt and dragged him closer until he was right in his face. "There's nothing for Caroline's parents to hear."

"Perhaps not, but you know how gossip is around

Cantara Hills. Hard to keep a secret. Now, if you'll quit manhandling me, Sergeant Caldwell, I'll tell you what you want to know about Kimberly McQuade."

"What about her?" And Egan didn't ask nicely, either.

But Carlson didn't speak until Egan released the grip he had on him. "Miles Landis said you were asking about Kimberly's lover."

"So?" Even from across the room, Caroline could see Egan's jaw tighten.

"Soooo, I know who he is."

Carlson didn't say more. Probably because someone came into the office and spoke Egan's name. Caroline recognized that voice, too. It was Lt. Brody McQuade, apparently back from his trip to California.

"What's going on here?" Brody asked.

Egan didn't take his eyes off Carlson. "Carlson was about to tell me the name of Kimberly's secret lover."

Brody came to the doorway. He glanced around. First at Egan. Then he spotted her. Brody no doubt noticed what Carlson already had, and she felt uncomfortable under his brief scrutinizing gaze.

"Welcome back, Lt. McQuade," Carlson greeted. It was syrupy sweet and sickening. He obviously detested Brody as much as he did Egan. "And how's your lovely fiancée, Victoria?"

"She's fine and with a bodyguard. Since I'm anxious to get back to her, I'd rather cut the BS. If you know something about Kimberly's affair, then spill it now or I'll just arrest you for obstruction of justice."

"Oh, I have no desire to keep this to myself. Miles won't mind if I share with you what he told me. Call it a guilty pleasure, but I'd love to see you Rangers at each others' throats, and news like this will do it. Maybe if you're fighting among yourselves, you'll leave the good citizens of Cantana Hills, me included, alone."

Egan got in Carlson's face. "Miles said he didn't know anything about her lover."

"Miles was a little, well, wasted, when he was in here. You just have to keep pushing, and it's amazing what he can remember. For instance, he recalled hearing a phone conversation."

"And?" Egan snarled when Carlson didn't immediately add anything.

"Miles overheard Kimberly talking to her lover. She was confused about her feelings."

Egan grabbed him by the shirt again. "I want a name, and I want it now. Tell me who her lover was."

Carlson's smile took on a sick, dangerous edge. "Well, it's none other than your fellow Texas Ranger, Sgt. Hayes Keller."

Chapter Eleven

Egan let go of Carlson and shook his head. He was about to tell Carlson that accusing Hayes of being Kimberly's secret lover was a sick joke.

But from Carlson's expression, he wasn't joking.

Carlson stepped back and straightened his clothes. "I'll give you all some privacy so you can discuss this Ranger-to-Ranger." He tossed one last glance at Caroline. "When I talk to your parents, I'll tell them you said hello."

"Please do," Caroline jabbed right back. She was glaring at Carlson when she walked closer. "And when I talk to them, I'll remind them that you're an ass. Oh, and if you call them to gossip, I'll have my own little chat with your boss. I know for a fact all employees here at the country club sign a confidentiality statement. Gossip won't be tolerated, even if that gossip might be true."

"You wouldn't have me fired," Carlson snarled.

"If she doesn't, I will," Egan volunteered.

Carlson gave Caroline a look meant to kill.

Egan wanted to pound Carlson to dust for that look and for saying those things about her. And for that other accusation against Hayes. But he didn't have time. Hayes came into the office, and he had a surveillance disk in his hand.

"Good news," Hayes announced, smiling. "The camera outside tennis boy's office wasn't working, but the one just up the hall is. We've got surveillance footage of the time before, during and after the shooting."

Egan saw just a split-second of what appeared to be concern in Carlson's eyes. But Egan didn't have time to deal with that now. He had a more pressing problem on his hands.

Hayes's smile faded. "What's going on?"

Brody and Egan exchanged glances. A dozen things passed between them, and none of those things were good. For starters, they had to ask Hayes what would have been unthinkable just minutes earlier.

"I'll excuse myself," Carlson said. "Obviously you have some business to discuss."

Egan grabbed his arm again. "This isn't over. And if you call Caroline's parents, you're going to regret it."

"Ohhhh." Carlson made a show of being afraid. "And what will you do?"

"I'll come after you." And Egan meant it. He had no doubts that his tone and expression conveyed that.

Carlson dropped the gleeful expression, and Egan got a glimpse of the raw anger lurking just beneath the surface. "Egan Caldwell, I'll see you dead before I let you put your low-rent hands on me again."

But it was Carlson who was shaking when he stormed out.

Egan didn't say anything else until Carlson and the guard were out of the room. Then he shut the door. Best to just put it all out there and get it resolved. "Carlson's stirring up trouble," Egan explained to Hayes. "He said you were the one having an affair with Brody's sister."

Egan expected Hayes to deny it. That they'd all share a laugh and curse Carlson for the petty lie he'd just told.

But Hayes didn't deny anything.

Egan's heart went to his knees. Judging from Brody's silence he was having the same reaction. Or worse.

"It just happened," Hayes said. He laid the surveillance disk on the desk. "Kimberly and I didn't plan it. She came to my place one night. She was upset. We had a few drinks…"

"Any reason you didn't tell us this sooner?" Brody's voice was low, intense and dangerous.

"I know, I should have." A moment later, Hayes repeated it. He groaned, sat down and put his face in his hands. "But I didn't know how, and Kimberly wanted to keep it a secret until we'd worked out our feelings for each other."

Hell. This was not what Egan wanted to hear. "Why not tell us after she was killed?"

"Because it wasn't pertinent to the investigation."

The look that went through Brody's eyes was dangerous. "You should have let me decide that."

Brody had said exactly what Egan was thinking. However, after what had just happened in the bedroom with Caroline, Egan was at least a little sympathetic to giving in to forbidden temptations.

But this?

Hayes had crossed a line by essentially withholding information. "Please tell me you haven't kept anything else a secret." Egan couldn't help but make it seem like an accusation.

Hayes pulled his hands from his face and stood. There

was some fire in his eyes, too. "You'd better not be suggesting I had anything to do with her death."

"Just asking." Egan had a tough time hanging on to his temper. Hayes was a fellow peace officer. Someone he'd grown up with. Gone to school with. A friend.

It seemed to take Hayes a moment to get his teeth unclenched. "You shouldn't have to ask. You know I wouldn't do anything to hurt Kimberly or any other woman."

"How would I know that?" It was Brody's turn to go on the attack. "You kept your affair secret."

Hayes lifted his hands, palms up, in the air and got back on his feet. "Because I knew this was how you'd act if you found out."

"I have a right to act this way." Brody's index finger landed on Hayes's chest. "Did you seduce her?"

"No." Though Hayes said it quietly, his voice was filled with emotion. And a warning—for Egan and Brody to back off. "She came on to me."

That wasn't the right answer because Brody charged at Hayes. He grabbed Hayes's shirt and shoved him against the wall.

Egan didn't know who was more surprised, Hayes or him. Brody had always been intense but never much of a physical fighter. No, the fights had usually erupted between Hayes and Egan. Childhood squabbles they'd settled with their fists and then gotten over it.

But Egan wasn't sure even a good fight would resolve this.

"Stop it!" Caroline yelled. Despite the fact that fists were about to be thrown, Caroline got between Brody and Hayes. "Go to your separate corners, guys, and cool off. I'm not going to let you beat each other senseless."

Surprisingly, Hayes and Brody stopped, even though their panting and angry stares meant this wasn't over.

"Carlson wants all of you at odds," Caroline announced.

She was right, of course. Carlson did want them at each other's throats. Why? Maybe to cover up that little detail about his testing positive for gunshot residue. And he didn't have an alibi for the shooting.

"Carlson might be the killer," Egan reminded Brody and Hayes. While he was at it, he reminded himself.

His gaze landed on the surveillance tape that Hayes had found, and he remembered Carlson's brief but intense reaction to it. "And there might be something on that tape to prove it."

CAROLINE SIPPED her morning coffee during her phone conversation with the antique broker from upstate New York. With everything else going on in her life, it wasn't exactly a conversation she wanted to have right now, but she was on the verge of a huge deal with this broker, and even with the murder attempts, she had to take care of her family's business. In this case, that meant rescheduling a meeting to sign the final paperwork that would seal the deal.

The broker wasn't happy with the delay; she could tell from his tone when he uttered a terse goodbye and hung up.

Heck, she wasn't happy, either. But leaving Egan's suite at Cantara Hills to go to her lawyer's office in downtown San Antonio just wasn't a smart idea. Nor did she want her lawyer to come to her because of the potential risk to him if he happened to get in the way of another attempt to kill her. She was feeling a lot like Typhoid Mary.

Besides, until the gunman/killer was caught, Egan

probably wouldn't let her leave, nor have visitors. He certainly seemed to be guarding the door to the suite. In fact, that's where he'd spent the night—in a chair bracketed right in front of the door while she took his bed.

Of course, neither of them had gotten much sleep.

At least she wasn't still having to wear his boxers and shirt. Along with the breakfast delivered to the suite, clothes for her had also arrived. Egan had sent one of the security guards to her house to get an outfit and her toiletries.

The guard had chosen a white knee-length bohemian skirt and a garnet-red tank top. Not exactly work attire, especially since they'd brought her funky jeweled flip-flops as well, but it beat the alternative. Everyone who'd seen her in Egan's boxers and shirt had assumed she'd had sex with the undergarment's owner. Which she hadn't. Well, unless that old analogy was correct—that a little bit of sex was like being a little bit pregnant. Degrees didn't matter.

The intimacy had been there.

And speaking of her partner in intimacy—like her, Egan was now involved with work. He was at the desk in the corner talking on the phone to someone at the Ranger Crime Lab in Austin while he continued to review the surveillance disk that Hayes had located. There were images taken on the day of her break-in and on the day of the shooting. And there were a lot of frames that included Carlson Woodward.

"Carlson," she mumbled under her breath. He'd likely phoned her parents by then. He was her parents' tennis instructor, and even though they were far from being best friends, they did talk and had occasionally gone out to lunch together. Carlson would use that connection to phone them and see what kind of trouble he could stir up. Because he probably thought the more trouble he caused, the harder it would be for Egan and the investigation.

If Carlson had indeed phoned them, her parents had likely tried to call her. There'd be messages on her still-missing cell phone. More messages at her house. And she was betting they had called friends and neighbors. She couldn't put off talking to her parents much longer, but she wanted to wait until she at least had some good news.

Judging from Egan's body language, that wasn't going to happen any time soon.

So, she bit the bullet and called to access her messages from her home phone.

First message, from her parents: "Caroline, Kenneth told us about the shooting. Call us now."

Second message: it was also from her parents. Her mother this time, and the gist, the same—call them.

Message three through eight were repeats of the same. But nine was the message she'd been expecting. And dreading.

"Caroline, this is your father, and I need to talk to you. Carlson called with some disturbing news about you and one of those Texas Rangers. Carlson said he was doing me a favor, that he was sure I wanted to know. Well, I do, but the news should have come from my daughter and not my tennis pro. I've already phoned the club manager, and he knows I'm not pleased about having Carlson Woodward, his employee, contact me about a private matter."

Sweet heaven. Carlson had done it. But she wasn't

going to take this lying down. She immediately called the concierge, who in turn put her through to the club manager, Michael DeCalley, an old friend of her father's. Michael informed her that based on the conversation he'd had with her father, he intended to talk to Carlson and that it was entirely possible that he would terminate Carlson's employment.

Caroline didn't feel any guilt at all about Carlson's losing his job. After the turmoil the man had gleefully created the night before, he deserved what he got. Plus, this would mean he wouldn't have access to Cantara Hills.

One less suspect who'd have the run of the place.

"Thanks," she heard Egan say to the caller on his phone. Egan hung up and glanced back at her. "Hayes collected the eavesdropping device from your house earlier and drove it to the crime lab in Austin."

She didn't miss the cool way he'd said his fellow Ranger's name. Obviously, Egan was still riled that Hayes hadn't been forthright about the secret affair with Kimberly.

"The lab just examined it…" Egan continued "…and were able to determine that it hadn't been left there the night of your break-in. The level of fine dust particles that had collected on it indicated it'd probably been there at least a week."

Caroline wanted to curse. For at least a week or more, she'd had no privacy whatsoever. "I guess there were no fingerprints to tell us who put it there?" And whoever it was, she wanted to throttle them.

"No fingerprints."

Of course not. It couldn't be that easy.

"Was the crime lab able to tell who was on the receiving end of the eavesdropping?" she asked.

Egan shook his head. "It wasn't a cheap device. Top of the line, actually. It had a quarter of a mile range for reception."

That both alarmed her and gave her some hope. "I have only five or six neighbors who live within a quarter of a mile of me."

That obviously wasn't new information to him. "Your parents, Taylor, Kenneth and Tammy Sutton, and your parents' best friends, the Jenkins."

Caroline nodded. "So, we're back to Kenneth and Tammy Sutton?"

"Not necessarily. The eavesdropping device could have been transmitting to a remote receiver, one that'd been planted somewhere near your house. That transmitter could have in turn fed the info to a receiver farther than a quarter of a mile away. Much farther."

Now she cursed under her breath. They hadn't narrowed down anything. The killer could be anywhere in Cantara Hills, or merely have access to it.

Which brought her to something she needed to tell Egan. "A little while ago, Taylor called. Her security guru is over at my house now, changing all the locks and updating my security system. I hope that won't interfere with your investigation."

"No. Actually, I think it's a good idea. The CSI guys are checking the grounds, of course, but there isn't any reason for them to go back in your house just yet because they've already processed it."

Egan paused the surveillance frames and whirled his chair around so they were facing. But he was a good twenty feet away, and he'd kept his distance since the "incident" the night before.

"So, think back to the past two weeks. Who's visited your house?" he asked. "And who would have had access to the kitchen?"

So they were back to more questions. Official ones. Where Egan was all Ranger.

She sipped her coffee while she gave that official question some thought. "My parents visited, of course. So did Kenneth and Tammy. Taylor, too. She comes over nearly every day. But I don't suspect her," Caroline quickly added.

"Neither do I. But what about her brother, Miles, and Carlson? Have they visited recently?"

"Unfortunately, yes." Why she hadn't thought of it sooner, she didn't know. Caroline stood and walked closer. "About a week and a half ago, maybe, Miles came by to ask if I knew where Taylor was, and Carlson was with him."

Egan groaned softly. "Let me guess—they came into your kitchen?"

She nodded. "Miles wanted to take some meds for a headache, or so he said, and he followed me into the kitchen for a glass of water."

"How about Carlson? Was he in the kitchen, too?" Egan asked.

It took her a moment to replay the events of that night. "Yes. He came in with Miles. And either of them could have planted the device because my back was to them for several seconds while I was at the fridge getting the water."

"It wouldn't have taken much effort. The device comes

with adhesive. And we already know Carlson's capable of doing something like this."

Oh, yes. He was capable of anything petty and nasty. But murder? She wasn't sure about that.

"Do you know if Carlson called your parents yet?" Egan wanted to know.

"He did." She drank more coffee. Avoided eye contact with him. "I'm sure they'll want to talk to me when they get back from their trip. But that's four days away." She'd have plenty of time to rehearse what she was going to say to assure them that she knew what she was doing.

Maybe during that time she could assure herself, too.

"Carlson's right about one thing," Egan continued. "Your parents will be upset. To them, I'm the equivalent of that vintage chopper you have hidden away in your garage. Fast and dangerous."

Caroline shrugged, tried to look flippant and walked even closer. "They don't want me to get hurt."

He caught her gaze. "Then you should keep your distance because with me, you will get hurt."

That was the first and only personal thing he'd said to her all night and morning. Too bad it had some merit. Merit that seemed way too serious for her already serious mood.

Trying to keep things light, Caroline gave his arm a gentle pinch. "You're like a truffle, Egan Caldwell. All solid on the outside, but I'm betting inside, there's a creamy soft filling."

She would have preferred a counter comment about his lack of richness, or something. Instead, he looked at her as if she'd missed a dose of meds and turned his attention back to the surveillance images. "Don't bet on that."

"Right. You're the guy who's never said I love you." Caroline chuckled. Not from humor. This conversation was too close to what they'd both been tiptoeing around for hours. Still, she didn't hush. The wound was there, and she had to examine it, even if she knew it was better off left alone. "My ex-fiancé used to say I love you all the time, and look how that turned out."

Egan turned back around and Caroline could almost read his mind. He was silently saying that it would turn out equally bad with him.

Or worse.

Again, he was right. But why did she want to be wrong? And then it hit her. With her mouth filled with coffee, it occurred to her that she was falling for Egan.

Really falling.

Well, damn. This couldn't happen. It just couldn't. When this investigation was over, she'd have to kiss Egan goodbye, and he'd go back to his office in Austin. That would be the end of it.

Wouldn't it?

She was still debating that when she realized something other than her had caught Egan's attention. He was leaning closer to the computer screen, where he was studying a still image on the surveillance disk.

It was Carlson Woodward.

"This footage was filmed about an hour before you arrived home and realized you had an intruder," Egan explained.

Caroline walked closer to get a better look. Yes, it was Carlson all right. He wore his usual tennis clothes and was coming out of the locker room. He had a gym bag clutched in his left hand.

"What do you see?" she asked Egan.

He tapped the gym bag. It was unzipped, and she could just make out a pair of shoes tucked inside.

Almost frantically, Egan used the keyboard to adjust the image. He zoomed in. And they got a much better look at the shoes.

"Those are Razors," he insisted. "The same type of shoes your intruder was wearing."

Oh, mercy. Was this the smoking gun? But then she looked closer. "There's a name or something on the tennis bag."

More key strokes, and Egan zoomed in on the monogram at the center, near the top zipper. The initials were MAL.

"Miles Andrew Landis," Caroline provided. "That's not even Carlson's bag."

He grunted in frustration. "So, why would Carlson have Miles Landis's bag?"

Caroline could think of a reason. "Miles plays tennis at the country club. Well, he does when he's sober. Maybe he left it in the locker room. Of course, if you question Carlson, he'll probably say he found it and was just returning it to Miles. He certainly wouldn't admit he'd planned to wear those shoes and break into my house to steal a dream journal."

"No. And Miles will likely claim he doesn't remember." Egan paused a moment. "I need answers about Miles because he seems to be the key to information we need."

She couldn't disagree with that. "What do you have in mind?"

"How about we ask Taylor to come down to the country club for a visit?" he asked, reaching for the phone.

"Any chance we can drive up to see her? Then, I can

stop by my house and get some things." Like a different set of clothes and a pair of more practical shoes.

He eased the phone back into its cradle. "I don't want you out in the open."

He had a point. She hopefully had a solution because she had major cabin fever and wanted to get out of there. "We could call ahead and park in Taylor's garage. We could do the same at my place. That way, we could walk directly into the houses. No being out in the open."

Again, he gave that some thought before he finally nodded. "Okay. Let's go talk to Taylor and ask her if she thinks her brother is capable of murder."

Chapter Twelve

Egan made Caroline's trek to the vehicle as fast as he could manage. He had his Jeep parked directly in front of the country club, and with his arm around Caroline, they practically ran to the vehicle so they could make the short drive to Taylor's.

He hoped to hell this wasn't a mistake.

All things considered, he would have preferred to keep Caroline locked away so the killer couldn't get to her. But the truth was, she might not even be safe at the country club. After all, the suite had windows, and there were no guarantees that the killer couldn't break in. The only thing he could do was continue to put himself between her and whoever this monster was who wanted her dead.

"Taylor moved her car out of the garage," Caroline relayed to Egan after a brief call to her friend. "When we get there, just pull into the empty space."

He nodded and started the drive up the winding hill. Taylor's house wasn't far, less than two miles, but each passing second only escalated his concern—and raised it even higher when a car burst out of a side street.

Egan slammed on the brakes, gave the steering wheel

a sharp turn to avoid a collision and reached for his gun. But he realized a gun wasn't necessary. The driver was a teenage boy with short, spiky black hair, and he gave them an indignant wave before he sped off.

"Wait a minute," Caroline insisted when Egan started to move again.

He glanced at her and saw that the color had drained from her face. "What's the matter?"

"I remember something about the hit-and-run. I remember Vincent Montoya."

All right. The timing was bad with them out in the open, but the shrink had said her memories might return. "What about him?" He volleyed glances between her and their surroundings. Even though this memory could be critical, he couldn't risk their being ambushed.

"Because of a streetlight, I saw his face. Right before he rammed into my car. I saw him. God, Egan." She started to tremble, and he slid his arm around her. "That wasn't the face of an angry man. But a determined one. Cold, unfeeling. Like a shark sitting there waiting to attack."

So Kimberly's death had likely been just a job to Montoya. That confirmed what Egan had already suspected. Now, the question was—who had hired Montoya to do that?

Egan glanced around them again and saw the car approaching from behind. The road was too curvy for the vehicle to pass, which meant he needed to get moving. Besides, he didn't like sitting there where anything could happen.

Even though Caroline was clearly upset, he eased his arm from her and continued the drive. "Do you remember anything else?" It was better to get her to focus on the details rather than the emotion, but Egan wasn't sure he could accomplish that just by getting her to talk about it.

She shook her head. "It was a flash, a quick glimpse of his face."

"But this is a good sign. You've remembered most of the accident now. And the parts you can't remember, that's because you were unconscious."

"Yes." She paused. "And those memories still haven't gotten us closer to the killer."

"You're wrong. Because of you, we know about Kimberly's argument with Kenneth, and we know Kenneth either lied or was mistaken about Montoya's motives. Montoya didn't kill Kimberly because she rejected his advances. He killed her because someone hired him to do that."

Caroline's breath shuddered. "And the person who hired him could be…anyone," she concluded with a heavy sigh.

No. Not just anyone. The list of suspects was pretty solid. Kenneth, Tammy, Carlson and Miles. Now, he needed to look for the link between these four and Montoya and Kimberly. Once he had the motive for Kimberly's death, then he would know the identity of the killer.

Egan turned into the stone-and-brick driveway. Taylor's car was parked on the side of her sprawling southwestern-style house, right next to the open garage. There was indeed a space waiting for them. So was Taylor. The slender blonde was in the doorway that led into the house, and as soon as Egan turned off the engine, she pressed the button to close the garage doors.

"Are you okay?" he asked Caroline as they got out of his Jeep.

She nodded, but he could tell that her nod was a lie.

The memory of Montoya had shaken her and this on the heels of the attempt to shoot her.

Taylor and Caroline hugged each other, and Taylor's gaze met his. It was a question—how's Caroline holding up? Egan only shrugged.

"Come in," Taylor invited, ushering them into a garden room just off the kitchen. She wore a perfectly tailored royal-blue business suit and heels.

"Thanks for delaying your business meeting," Caroline said.

"Don't worry about it. I told the bank trustees that I'd be about a half hour late. I hope that'll be enough time for our chat."

"It will be," Caroline assured her. "We only have a few questions."

True. But they were potentially volatile.

A gleaming silver tray of coffee was waiting for them on a granite-and-glass table, and both Caroline and he sat in the white wicker chairs and helped themselves to cups of the brew.

"This is about your brother," Egan started.

"I figured as much. I heard about the search warrant and the shoes taken from his condo. Please tell me those shoes didn't match the prints left by the intruder on Caroline's bedroom floor."

"They didn't. But that doesn't rule him out."

Taylor nodded. "Because he could have gotten rid of them." She reached out and gently touched Caroline's hand. "I'm so sorry if Miles is responsible for any of what's happened to you."

"I know. But you're not his keeper. You don't have to apologize for him."

Egan was relieved. Judging from Taylor's comment and attitude, she might not get defensive about his next question. "Do you think Miles might have had something to do with Kimberly McQuade's death?"

Taylor's only reaction was that she blew out a long breath. "I wish I could say no, but I've been thinking about this. No proof, just a theory. Miles and Montoya weren't friends, exactly, but I know that Montoya loaned some money to my brother. And I'm sure it was a sizeable amount. Maybe the hit-and-run had something to do with that?"

Egan couldn't see an immediate connection, but he'd dig deeper. "But what about what's happened recently? Have you seen or heard anything to indicate that Miles wants Caroline dead?"

"Nothing." Her answer was fast, which meant Taylor had likely given it some thought as well. "I know he asks her for loans all the time, but he's never had anything bad to say about her."

"What about anyone else?" Caroline asked. "Have you noticed anything about Kenneth, for instance, that would make you think he's involved?"

"No."

"I remembered seeing Kimberly and Kenneth argue the night of your Christmas party," Caroline volunteered.

"Oh, yes. That," Taylor agreed. "I remember it, too. They were in the corridor of the guest wing. I walked by there, heard voices and opened the doors. There they were."

This was the first Egan had heard of this. "Why didn't you tell us sooner?"

Taylor dismissed it with a head shake. "Because I didn't remember it until you asked. You think it's important?"

"Could be." And it brought them back to Kenneth, again.

"I didn't actually hear anything they said," Taylor continued. "In fact, I can't even be sure it was an argument. They looked intense. But it could have been they were just discussing business."

Egan doubted that.

"I didn't hear the argument, either," Caroline added a moment later. "But I remember that Kimberly was upset with Kenneth and she wouldn't say why."

"That's not usual. Kenneth can rub people the wrong way. Sometimes ambition doesn't leave a lot of room for tact." Taylor poured herself some coffee. "I take it he's a suspect?"

Egan avoided the question. He glanced at both of them. "I want you both to think back to the night of the party. Was there anything unusual going on at the City Board or here in Cantara Hills?"

After several moments, Caroline spoke up. "I think it was just normal business at the City Board. There was a big contract bid that was about to be revealed. But that was it."

. "And as for here in the neighborhood…" Taylor answered "…there was the party here at my house, of course. It wasn't just a Christmas party. It was to celebrate the recent success of the City Board."

Yes. Egan had looked into that success. Funds, a huge amount, had recently been approved to build a new west-side library and extend the tourist area of the Riverwalk, the main artery of the thriving downtown area. But Egan hadn't found anything about that to tie to the murders.

Maybe it was time to take another look.

"I'll go over all the City Board records for that time period," Egan explained. He stood. "Maybe something will turn up."

Caroline stood as well. The two women shared another hug. "I'm worried about you," Taylor whispered.

"You don't have to be. I'm in good hands."

That sent Taylor's gaze sliding his way. But not just a gaze. A friend's scrutinizing one. Egan silently cursed. What, were Caroline and he wearing god-awful big signs on their foreheads so that anyone near them could read that they were attracted to each other?

Egan vowed then and there to focus just on the investigation. But one look at Caroline, at her sleep-starved eyes and her too-pale skin, and he knew he was kidding himself. He couldn't keep his mind off her for even a minute.

Somehow, he'd have to deal with that.

"If I remember anything else, I'll give you a call," Taylor assured them. She followed them out of the garden room and back to the garage. When she got to the exit, she pressed the button again to open the doors.

"Do your parents know?" Taylor asked Caroline.

Caroline didn't say "about what?" She merely sent a warm glance his way. "Probably."

"So you haven't talked to them about Egan," Taylor clarified.

Caroline shook her head.

"My advice—you'd better. Tammy called this morning with the latest gossip. You two are the hot topic of Cantara Hills. The chauffeur's son and the socialite. Everyone thinks you're having an affair."

"Do they now?" Caroline mumbled. There was no weary breath or heavy sigh. Nor did she look uncomfortable.

Probably because there was nothing she could do about it. Carlson had already spilled everything to her parents.

"Be careful," Taylor added, and she gave Caroline another hug before closing the door.

"Gossip," Egan repeated under his breath. "That, and your parents' reaction to an involvement with me are two Texas-size reasons for me to keep my hands off you."

He sounded like he was trying to convince himself.

He was.

"Your *hands?*" Caroline questioned. The slight smile she sent his way let him know that it wasn't his "hands" they had to worry about.

Egan scowled, knowing it was true, and he headed for the Jeep. He made it only one step when the explosion ripped through the garage.

IT WAS HAPPENING ALL OVER again.

At the sound of the explosion, Caroline instinctively tried to drop to the ground. Thanks to Egan and the impact of the blast itself, that wasn't a problem. Both of them ended up on the garage floor, and both of them were pelted with flying debris.

Caroline caught just a glimpse of the source. Or rather what remained of the source.

It was Taylor's car. The car she'd parked outside the garage so that Egan could park inside.

So they'd be safe.

There wasn't much left of Taylor's vehicle. It had literally been blown apart and was now on fire. Black coils of smoke rose from it, smearing into the air. Stench from the burning leather seats and rubber tires boiled into the garage, and Caroline couldn't breathe.

The door between the house and garage flew open, and Taylor gasped when she looked out. "My God, are you hurt?" She proceeded to drag them aside.

Caroline and Egan went willingly. She wanted to put as much distance as possible between them and that fireball in Taylor's side yard.

"We need to move away from the garage," Egan ordered. He grabbed on to both Taylor and her, and they raced to the other end of the house.

Once he had them shoved into the library, he drew his gun and his cell phone. "Hayes," Caroline heard him say after he pressed in some numbers. "I need backup at Taylor Landis's house. There's been another explosion. Caroline and I have only been here fifteen minutes, so the perp might still be around. Come, and bring Brody."

Caroline's stomach twisted into a knot. *Not again. Please, don't let this be happening again.* She grabbed Taylor and moved her away from the window.

Egan stayed at the door, looking out. He had a firm grip on his gun. "Taylor, is your security system armed?"

"Just for the windows. I disengaged the doors when I let you in."

Oh, mercy. That meant someone could be walking right into the house. Or could already be inside.

Egan obviously realized the same thing because he glanced around the room. "Get under the desk," he insisted.

They didn't argue. Caroline and Taylor hurried to the massive oak desk and climbed under it. Egan locked the library door and went to the window to stand guard.

"Do you see anyone?" Caroline asked.

"No."

But that didn't mean *someone* wasn't there.

Had the killer planted that bomb while Egan and she were inside talking? If they'd stayed just another minute, Egan would have been backing out when the explosive device detonated.

They would have probably been killed.

"Caroline, check and make sure you aren't hurt," Egan called back to her.

She hadn't even thought of that, and she was probably too numb and in shock to feel actual pain. She held out her hands. No injuries. And she looked at Taylor, who reached out and wiped something from Caroline's cheek.

Blood.

"It's just a scratch," Taylor whispered.

Caroline quickly tried to clean it all off. She wanted no trace of blood because she knew that would only incense Egan. She didn't want him going after this vile creature. Without backup, it could be suicide.

And then it hit her.

"Egan, are you hurt?" she asked.

"No."

But he wasn't telling the truth. She saw the trickle of blood making its way from his forehead down his cheek. Caroline started to go to him, but Taylor stopped her. "Not now," Taylor said.

Her friend was right, but it took every ounce of Caroline's willpower to stay put and not try to make sure that cut wasn't the only injury he had.

"Taylor, any chance you have surveillance cameras around the garage area?" Egan asked.

"Sorry, no."

So there'd be no footage of someone setting the bomb. Their only chance would be to find some kind of evidence he'd left behind. But if this bomber was also her intruder, then he had already left so much with those tracks on her floor, and they hadn't caught him yet.

Furious at not being able to do anything, Caroline reached up and grabbed the phone from Taylor's desk so she could make a call. To Kenneth. To his personal cell phone. She pressed in the numbers. Waited.

But there was no answer.

Of course, that didn't prove anything, but it certainly made her consider if he could be out there running away from an explosion he'd set.

"Call Miles," Caroline said, thrusting the phone at Taylor. "See if he answers."

Almost frantically, Taylor punched in the numbers, and a moment later, she shook her head. "It went straight to voice mail."

"How about Carlson?" Caroline asked. "Do you have his number?"

Taylor scanned through the index function on her phone and nodded. She pressed the key to automatically dial it and then put in on speaker so they'd all be able to hear what he said.

"Taylor," Carlson answered, obviously seeing her number on his caller ID. "To what do I owe this call?"

He seemed distracted and out of breath, and Caroline didn't think it was her imagination. Apparently, Egan felt the same way because he cursed under his breath.

"I dialed the wrong number," Taylor told him, probably because she didn't know what else to say.

"You're sure? You're not having any problems there, are you? Because I don't mind coming over to check on you."

Carlson not only sounded out of breath and distracted,

he somehow managed to sound a little smug. Caroline wished she could reach through the phone and smack him.

God, had he been the one to set that bomb?

Had his pettiness gone this far?

Caroline remembered what Egan had told her about the man. Carlson had tormented a pet, all because he didn't like Egan. Cruelty to animals was a sign of deviant and even dangerous behavior. Was he capable of doing something even more sinister now that he was an adult?

"No problems here," Taylor lied to Carlson, and she hung up.

"Carlson needs to be questioned," Caroline relayed to Egan.

"Yeah. I heard."

Outside, she could hear the sirens, indicating the Rangers were getting closer. Inside, Egan's phone rang. Caroline listened, hoping that it was someone calling to say they'd captured the person responsible. But judging from Egan's body language, that hadn't happened.

"Brody, Hayes and the guards are outside," he relayed. "They don't see anyone."

"So, what do we do?" Taylor asked.

"Come on. We're getting out of here. It's not safe because there might be another bomb."

Chapter Thirteen

From the driveway of Caroline's house, Egan sat in the bulletproof CSI vehicle and watched the activity. Something he'd been doing all afternoon and something that he would continue to do deep into the night.

And Caroline was in his arms.

With her head on his shoulder.

Egan hadn't even tried to put some distance between them, either physical or otherwise. This was the third attempt in just as many days to kill her, and Caroline was rightfully upset. If being in his arms seemed to soothe her, then that's where she would stay.

To hell with regulations and protocol.

The bomb squad had finished with Taylor's house and hadn't found a second explosive device. Now, they had gone over to Caroline's, just in case the killer had decided to hit her property for a second round. For over an hour, the squad had been in her house to search every inch of it with dogs and equipment, but they were now trickling out and heading for their respective vehicles.

"It doesn't look as if they found anything," Caroline commented.

Even though her head was on his shoulder, her attention was glued to her house. Like Egan, for the past hour she'd no doubt been holding her breath, waiting to see if it, too, would explode.

So far, so good.

The remainder of the bomb squad came out, leaving only Hayes inside to do the final wrap-up.

The medics had already tended to the cuts on his forehead and Caroline's cheek. She had a small white bandage angled just beneath her right eye. Egan could barely stand to look at it because it was a reminder of how close she'd come to being seriously hurt. Or worse.

"You think Taylor's okay?" Caroline asked, glancing over at her friend's house. The place had been marked off with yellow Do Not Cross tape that was fluttering in the summer breeze.

"Brody will see to her," Egan assured her.

But Egan doubted Taylor would be "okay" for a while. She was no doubt shaken to the core. Right now, Taylor was probably being interviewed, but once that was done, she'd be staying the night in Brody's own suite.

Just a precaution.

Egan and Caroline had almost certainly been the targets, but Taylor had been there, right along with them in the line of danger. Besides, Taylor probably wouldn't feel comfortable spending the night in her own home.

Hayes finally came out of the front door of Caroline's house, and she lifted her head and moved slightly away from Egan. For propriety's sake, no doubt.

"All clear. No additional bombs," Hayes announced, volleying his attention between Caroline and Egan. "We checked the security system—it's working. And like you requested, your security company put some motion activators around the exterior. If anyone comes near the place tonight, we'll know about it because it'll set off the alarms. If they're tripped, you'll be able to hear a series of beeps from inside the house."

Egan nodded. "Good. Thanks." At least they wouldn't be ambushed again.

"There's more," Hayes continued. "I had the security guards question the residents in the immediate area, and the Roberts just up the street said they saw Kenneth out for a jog. It was about two hours before the bomb went off. Ms. Roberts was in her rose garden, and she thinks Kenneth turned into Taylor's driveway."

Egan didn't like the sound of that. It put a prime suspect in the vicinity.

"Ms. Roberts was quick to say that she didn't think Kenneth would do anything wrong," Hayes added.

"Of course not," Egan mumbled. The residents would protect one of their own, even if that person was the one trying to kill Caroline.

Egan turned to Caroline. "Here's the plan. While Hayes transports some of this bomb evidence to the lab in Austin, you and I will wait in your house. With all the security updates, your place would be easier to keep safe than the suite at the country club." There were too many nooks and crannies there to set bombs, and the surveillance system seemed to be constantly malfunctioning. Or being tampered with.

"Then what?" she asked.

Egan took a deep breath, not knowing how she would react to what he was about to say. "Once he's back from Austin, which shouldn't take more than two to three hours, Hayes will stay here at the house with you tonight. You're in his protective custody now."

"I see." Which seemed to be another way of saying, *Egan, you're avoiding me.*

He was. Still, Egan wasn't under any illusions that avoiding her would make him want her less. But this way, he might be able to keep his focus and solve this case.

She glanced uneasily at Hayes and him. "Did you two mend fences with each other?"

"No," Hayes and Egan said quickly and in unison.

"But you will." She sighed.

The irritation was still too strong for Egan to admit that she was right. But, by God, Hayes had screwed up. Egan had wasted valuable time investigating Kimberly McQuade's so-called secret lover, a man he thought might be a killer. He could have used that time to find the real killer and therefore make Caroline safe.

Yeah. That was worth another day or two of irritation.

Egan and Hayes exchanged a rather frosty "See you later," and Egan pulled the car up close to the porch. As close as he could get to the steps.

"Go in your house as fast as you can," he instructed. She nodded, and they barreled out of the vehicle, both hurrying inside. Egan immediately double-locked the door and engaged the security system.

"Don't go near the windows," he added. He figured there'd be a lot of such warnings while he was with her. And confusion. Since the only place without windows was where they were standing.

Caroline didn't protest his orders. In fact, she didn't say anything. Neither did he. They just looked at each other.

That look. It needed no interpretation, and it was effective in making him more mindless than he already was.

Egan hooked his arm around her waist and pulled her to him.

And he kissed her.

He didn't even bother to try to stop himself. Egan needed to feel her against him if only for a couple of seconds. He made those seconds worth the risk. He took her mouth, letting the taste of her slide through him. But then, he let go and eased away from her.

She didn't hold on, but she did look at him as if he'd lost his mind. "This protective custody arrangement with Hayes is a matter of semantics," she accused.

Egan had anticipated this conversation. It had the potential to turn into an argument. Not necessarily a bad thing. Because anger might keep them apart.

Then he shook his head.

Nothing, perhaps not even paralysis or near death would keep them apart. He wanted her that much. And then there was the torturous ache. His body wanting hers.

Wait.

Not wanting her body. Wanting *her*. The subtle difference was massive, and Egan didn't even want to explore the implications of that.

"Maybe it's semantics to you," he said. He felt himself halving the already narrow space between them. "But there's paperwork that makes a protective custody arrangement legal."

She halved the half. Until her body was so close to his that he could feel the heat. And they were generating a hell of a lot of heat.

"So?" she challenged. "You think if you legally assign

me to someone else, then you can pretend that nothing happened in your suite last night?"

The question was solid, argumentative. But her tone was all silk, sex and fire. Then she made it worse by moistening her bottom lip with her tongue.

"Look," he started. But he had to stop. Because he'd lost his train of thought. Instead, he did something totally stupid. He reached out and slid his thumb through that moisture on her bottom lip. "Assigning you to Hayes is a way of relieving my guilt over wanting you. A way of keeping this badge on my chest."

She caught his hand to stop him from pulling it back. So his thumb stayed brushing against her lip. "That badge. My parents. Your crummy childhood. Our socio-economic backgrounds. Yes, we have more than enough reasons to forget what happened last night. And there's absolutely no logical reason to remember it, is there?"

And she waited. Staring at him.

Hell.

No logical reason. Plenty of the other variety, though. The illogical, emotionally career-suicidal reasons. But it was useless to try to think about them when his body and mind wanted only one thing.

Caroline.

He reached for her so fast that Egan saw the split-second of shock in her eyes. But it wasn't shock he heard in the throaty sound she made when he kissed her. That sound was approval, maybe even relief, and then moments later, absolute pleasure.

Without taking his mouth from hers, he pulled them against the door. His back hit hard, so hard that he'd have bruises. He didn't care. Nothing else mattered right then.

Her mouth was as hungry as his, and while he had his hands occupied with holding her, Caroline put her own fingers to good use. She went after his shirt.

Egan went after hers.

He wanted to take his time with her. To savor every bit of Caroline. But that was a pipe dream. There was only one way this could happen between them. Explosive and fast. They'd have to burn off some of this white-hot energy and need before they could get to the foreplay.

She jerked back the sides of his shirt. The badge, pinned to the shirt, clanged when it hit against the door. Egan knew that should have been a reminder of exactly what was at stake there, but a reminder wasn't going to stop him.

With her hands playing havoc on his bare chest, Egan shoved up her top. Her bra was all lace, barely there, and he unclipped the front hook and created some havoc of his own by taking her right nipple into his mouth.

She made another sound—a deep, rich moan—and melted against him. Egan savored her while Caroline obviously savored what he was doing.

But only for a few moments.

That nipple kiss only made the heat more impossible, and she began a war with his belt buckle and zipper.

Her eyes were wild, and even though her touches and kisses were blurring his vision, he savored the sight of her, too. She was amazing. Beautiful. With her face flushed with arousal.

Then she slid her hands into his jeans and sent the battle to the next level.

Egan had to take a deep breath just to try to clear his head. But her touch made a clear head impossible. She ran her hand down the length of him. By the time she finished, Egan had no self-control.

She smiled as if she knew exactly what she was doing to him. So Egan turned the tables on her. Pinning her against the door, he shoved up her loose white skirt. Found a pair of white lace panties that matched her bra. But he didn't take the time to appreciate her taste in underwear.

He put his fingers inside those panties, inside her.

No more smiling. She moaned. Gasped. Her eyelids fluttered. She let the door support the back of her head. And she angled her hips so that his fingers would go deeper into her. That seemed to satisfy her for a moment or two, but soon it obviously wasn't enough.

"Do something about this," she said.

Oh, he intended to do something. He wanted her so much that waiting was agony.

"Here?" Egan asked, already stripping off her panties.

"Here," Caroline insisted.

Good. Because they wouldn't have made it to the bed anyway. Egan wrapped her legs around him and freed himself from his boxers. Because they were practically eye-to-eye, he watched her as she took him inside her. Inch by inch. She was tight and wet, and the sensations of that intimate caress robbed him of what was left of his breath. He didn't care.

Compared to this, breathing was overrated.

He moved inside her. Caroline moved, too. Matching him thrust for thrust. She buried her fingers in his hair. Rocked against him. Man, she was a picture all right. The wild child. No inhibitions. No doubts about what she wanted from him.

Egan watched her get closer to the edge. Her eyes

shimmered and were on him, but with each now-frantic thrust, her vision became pinpointed, not on him, exactly, but on the release that was a necessity.

She said his name. *Egan*. Using that classy silk voice. First, just a whisper. She repeated it, and her voice drove him harder. Deeper. Faster.

Until she shattered.

Egan felt her close around him like a fist. He smelled her sex. And kissed her so he could taste her release. He hung on to each of those sensations as long as he could—which wasn't very long.

Caroline's climax brought on his. Egan could only do one thing: hold on tight and ride over that edge with her. It was a damn good ride, too.

She laughed. Part enjoyment. Part exhaustion. Part relief. He knew exactly how she felt.

"Did we survive?" she asked.

"I'm not sure." Either way, it'd been worth it.

Egan had to close his eyes a moment when the little aftershock of her climax gave him an aftershock of his own. She slid against him. Teasing him and herself in the process.

"That wasn't because you felt sorry for me," she insisted. Her breath was rough and jolted against his sweat-dampened face. She kissed him. And moved against him.

Hell. He was getting hard again.

"No." With her still pinned to the door, Egan slid them to the floor and disengaged. What he didn't do was let go of her. He kept here there in his arms. At the rate they were going, they'd have sex again in a few minutes anyway.

She latched on to his face and forced eye contact. "And it wasn't ordinary."

Egan didn't even consider lying. "No. It wasn't."

Caroline cocked her head to the side. And laughed again. That laughter probably would have initiated a conversation they should have—because he knew she wasn't the type to have casual sex. But his cell phone rang, the sound echoing through the foyer.

Egan let go of Caroline so that he could retrieve the phone from his pocket and answer it. The caller ID indicated it was Brody. *Great.* It wouldn't be an easy call to take just then. In other words, Egan had to sound as if he hadn't just had sex against the door with Caroline.

"Brody?" he answered. Caroline, obviously out of breath, rolled away from him and landed on a nearby area rug. No panties. Her skirt up around the tops of her thighs. And her breasts exposed for the taking.

He wanted her all over again.

"Anything wrong?" he asked Brody.

Brody didn't say anything for several seconds. "Are you all right? You sound funny."

Egan silently groaned. Sometimes, like now, he swore Brody had ESP. "I'm fine. Why'd you call?"

"The bomb squad just gave me a prelim report on that device that took out Taylor's car. Like the other one, it'd been set on a timer."

"That doesn't surprise me. The killer probably timed it when he thought Caroline and I would be in the garage. Or backing out of it."

"Not quite. The timer went off exactly when it was set to go off." Brody paused. "I don't think this bomb was meant for Caroline and you."

Egan quickly went through the details of that meeting with Taylor and came to the same conclusion. "Taylor delayed an appointment to see us. If she hadn't, she would have been in her car driving at the time the device detonated."

"That's what I think, too."

Oh, man. This was not a complication they needed. "So Taylor's a target now."

That brought Caroline off the floor, and the alarm was immediate in her eyes. "What happened to Taylor?"

"Nothing. She's all right." Egan relayed what Brody had just told him. Caroline's eyes registered the fear and concern as well.

"Once Hayes is back from Austin," Brody continued, "I'll bring Taylor to Caroline's. I think it's a good idea if both women are in protective custody."

It was a logical plan. Besides, it would free up Brody to keep a closer eye on his fiancée, Victoria, who perhaps was also still in danger from the Cantara Hills killer. Of course, with Taylor in the house, there'd be far less chance that he'd have sex with Caroline again.

Egan tried hard to see that as a plus.

It sure didn't feel like a plus.

Caroline got to her feet, put her panties back on and fixed her clothes. "I'll call Taylor and see how she's handling all of this."

He stood, too, zipping his jeans.

Just as the beeping sound began to pulse through the house.

It took Egan a moment to realize what was making that sound. It was the security system. Specifically, one of the motion-activated devices that had just been installed around the perimeter of the house.

Someone had set it off.

And that meant the killer could be out there, maybe trying to plant another bomb.

Egan checked the security keypad next to the front door. None of the indicator lights were on. So at least the killer wasn't inside, and he intended to keep it that way.

He took out his phone. "I need to call Brody and tell him what's going on."

But before he could press in a single number, the doorbell rang. Egan drew his weapon and stepped back, putting himself in front of Caroline.

"Who is it?" he called out.

No one answered right away, and that caused his heart rate to spike. It spiked even more when he heard the man's voice.

"This is Caroline's father. Let me in. I want to speak to my daughter *now.*"

Chapter Fourteen

Caroline thought there were few things worse than hiding out from a killer. However, facing her father definitely wasn't something she wanted to do mere minutes after having sex with Egan.

But she had no choice.

She'd have to let him in.

There was no way she could talk her father into coming back later after she'd composed herself. He'd heard of the attempts on her life from Kenneth. And of course, Carlson had made that call to tell them all about Egan and her.

"Let us in," her father insisted.

Us. So her mother was with him as well. Not surprising. They were joined at the hip when it came to matters pertaining to her.

"If you don't let us in, I'll use my key," her father threatened.

And he would, too—even though with the changed locks, the key she'd given him for emergencies would no longer work. That probably wouldn't stop him. Not because he delighted in invading her privacy, but in his frame of mind, he might think she was being held hostage or something else unsavory. He wouldn't be content until he could see her face-to-face.

"I'll be right there," Caroline answered in the calmest voice she could manage. She finished straightening her clothes and looked at Egan. "You might want to go in the bedroom and give me some alone time with my parents."

"Right," he said in a tone to indicate that wasn't going to happen.

"It won't be pleasant," she added. She only hoped the inevitable argument didn't turn physical. It wouldn't on Egan's or her part. He wouldn't lose his cool enough to take a swing at her father.

Caroline quickly finger-combed her hair and disengaged the security system. She gave Egan another look while her hand was poised on the door lock. "Last chance to escape."

Egan just shook his head. "I'm not leaving you alone to face this."

She hadn't expected that he would. Egan was a rescuer, with all those bad-boy traits. An odd combination. And an appealing one. He wouldn't hide behind her, and he wouldn't steal her parents' money.

But a broken heart was probably just on the horizon for her.

That didn't stop Caroline from brushing a kiss on his hot, surly mouth before she opened the door.

There they were. Her parents. And Egan's father, Walt. *Oh, great.*

"We figured it was a good idea for Walt Caldwell to be in on this," her father announced. "So we called Link and told him we wanted Walt to meet us here."

Caroline knew for a fact that idea wasn't good. Her

own parents were enough of a challenge without adding in Egan's dad.

"Well?" her father said. James Edward Stallings III was wearing khaki Bermuda shorts, brown leather sandals and an absurdly perky tropical shirt littered with exotic flowers. The perkiness didn't extend to his expression. He was scowling.

Her mother, Elaina, just looked concerned. Her normally perfect brunette bob was mussed, her makeup slightly smeared and her white linen dress wrinkled. Probably because they'd left their Cancun hotel room in a rush and hadn't stopped until they'd arrived on her doorstep.

In contrast, Walt looked as he always did. Dressed in his perfectly pressed chauffeur's uniform, he stood almost subserviently behind her parents and dodged her gaze completely.

"Are you all right?" her mother asked. "Kenneth said you weren't hurt in the explosion, but I had to see for myself."

"I'm okay. *Really,*" Caroline added when her mother frowned and gave her a questioning stare.

"If you're okay," her father pointed out, "then why the bandage on your cheek?"

Amazingly, she'd nearly forgotten about that. "Just a scratch. Truly, I'm fine. And while I'm sure you're concerned about my safety, I doubt that's the sole reason you're here, especially since Mr. Caldwell is with you."

"They say you're playing around with some big trouble, boy," Walt grumbled after no one else said anything.

Her father gave a stiff nod and glared at Egan.

Caroline's mom stepped in ahead of her husband as if to put herself between James and them. It wasn't necessary. Her father wouldn't hit her or anything, not even close. He wouldn't even raise his voice, to her, but her mom no doubt knew there was going to be an ugly argument.

There wasn't much chance of stopping that.

Caroline decided the best defense was a good offense, and the offense she had going for her was the truth. But where to start?

She took a deep breath. "Carlson called you because he wanted to cause trouble for Egan."

"Are you sleeping with Sgt. Caldwell?" Her father obviously bypassed her comment and went right to the heart of the matter.

"James!" her mother scolded.

Caroline put a hand on Egan's chest when he stepped forward. "Don't worry. I'm not going to answer that question because it's none of his business." She looked at her father. "I'm sorry, Dad, but you're not entitled to the details of my sex life." Then, she looked at Walt. "And for the record, neither are you."

"It's my business when your parents brought me in on this," Walt countered.

"And it's my business if you're going to get hurt," her father added.

Because there were beads of sweat rapidly popping out on her father's forehead and because he looked ready to implode, Caroline caught him by the arm and urged him inside. Walt followed, barely stepping inside, and Caroline shut the door. No sense airing their argument for the neighbors to hear, and at least this way the A/C would keep them physically cooler.

"I want you to calm down, James," her mother insisted.

Caroline nodded. "That's good advice. This isn't worth having another heart attack. Heck, it's not even worth this brouhaha you're causing." She felt Egan stiffen and looked at him. "I didn't mean it like that."

Crud. Now, she was upsetting everyone, including herself. "What I'm trying to say, and not saying it very well, is that Egan isn't a thief. He's a highly respected Texas Ranger with an incredible commitment to his badge."

"He had no right to get involved with you," Walt interjected.

Egan stepped closer to him. He stabbed his index finger at his father. "And you have no say in any part of my life."

"I do when you're screwing up. What you do with the likes of Caroline Stallings washes back on to me."

"Why? Because Link Hathaway and his cronies won't like it? And because you'd do anything to please your boss? What you and your boss think are not my problem."

Caroline was about to intercede. She wanted to defend Egan. To tell his father what a wonderful man he'd become despite the lack of attention from his parent. But after one glance at Egan, she knew he had to handle this by himself.

"Caroline Stallings is in the Rangers' protective custody," Egan calmly explained to his father. "That means I decide who comes in and who leaves. You're leaving."

Walt shook his head. "Not until you agree to keep your hands off her."

Egan latched on to his father's arm. Not roughly. And other than the iron set of his jaw, he showed no emotion. "I owe you no promises. Nor any agreements. But here's a promise—if you don't leave now, I'll have you arrested for hindering my investigation." With that, he opened the door and muscled his father onto the porch. Without so much as a glance, he shut the door.

The silence came. With all of them staring at each other.

"I'm sorry," Caroline said to Egan.

Egan shrugged. She didn't think it was an under-reaction, either. More like an acceptance that some relationships just couldn't be fixed.

"So you really are involved with Sergeant Caldwell?" her mother asked.

Silence met her question.

Not that Caroline expected Egan to supply some magic answer that would please everyone. But as the person who responded, it left her having to bare her soul. "I care for him, Mom."

There. She'd said it. A handful of words that would likely send Egan running because they smacked of commitment and other things he'd spent a lifetime avoiding.

More silence followed.

She didn't dare look at Egan. Instead, she kept her attention on her mother, who was the most likely ally Caroline had right now.

"I'm thirty years old," Caroline reminded her parents. Then, she told them something they probably didn't know. "I've been celibate for three years since that slime bucket, Julian, crushed my heart and robbed us blind. I gave up dating the kind of guys I like. I gave up sports cars. I work a sixty-hour week and don't take vacations. And I'm a little tired of playing it safe because safe isn't what I want."

She certainly knew how to shut down a conversation. She glanced at them, and at least they all appeared to be thinking about what she'd said.

"I'm worried you'll get hurt again," her father said.

Caroline turned her attention back to him. "I know. But

I'm not going to stop seeing Egan unless he wants to. He and I will be the ones who'll continue or end things between us. Not you, Mom and Dad, and not Walt Caldwell."

Glances were exchanged all around. Her father stared at Egan. "Did you sleep with her?"

"Yes," Egan admitted. "Not that it's any of your business, but I did. And now I suppose you're going to ask what my intentions are?"

Her father gave a too-stiff nod. "I am."

Could this get any more embarrassing? She felt like a schoolgirl who'd been caught stuffing her bra with toilet paper. "Don't answer that," she told Egan.

Egan didn't listen. "My intentions first and foremost are to protect her. I'm not interested in her money. Nor yours. I only want to catch a killer and put him behind bars so that Caroline will be safe."

Her father looked a little shocked with Egan's sincere explanation of his intentions. And perhaps because those intentions obviously didn't include anything personal. He made a sound that could have meant anything and reached for the doorknob.

"Call if you need us," her father instructed.

She released the breath she didn't even know she'd been holding. Then Caroline nodded, brushed kisses on both their cheeks. "I love you."

"We love you, too," her mom answered. A moment later, her dad echoed the same.

When they walked out, Caroline quickly closed the door, locked it and reset the security system. "I'm so sorry you had to go through that."

Egan stayed quiet a moment. "Even after the argument, you still told them you love them."

She blinked, surprised that after all she'd said that was the first thing he wanted to address. "Because I do love them. They're not bad people, Egan. They're just my parents, and they think if they can protect me from being hurt, then they've done their job."

He shook his head as if he didn't get that, maybe because he'd never been on the receiving end of any real parental affection.

"You've really been celibate for three years?" he asked.

Now *that* was one of the questions she had anticipated. "*Been* is the operative word. Obviously, my celibacy ended when I met you."

He shrugged uncomfortably, followed by another shake of his head. "Why?"

"Why what?" Best to clarify because it was a question that could get her in trouble.

"Why end your celibacy with me?"

She thought about it before she answered. "Because I was telling the truth when I said I really like you." To ease the tenseness in his face, she smiled and brushed a kiss on his mouth. "Don't worry, I'm not going to get all clingy."

Even if clingy suddenly didn't sound so bad.

Oh, mercy. She really was speeding her way to that broken heart.

The phone rang, and she automatically turned to answer it, but Egan caught her arm. "I don't want you near the windows," he reminded her. He went into the kitchen and came back with the cordless phone.

She glanced at the caller ID on the small screen. "It's Michael DeCalley, the manager of the Cantara Hills Country Club," she relayed to Egan.

"Caroline," Michael greeted her after she answered

the phone. Egan's phone rang as well, and he stepped a few yards away to take the call. "I just wanted you to know that I went ahead and talked with Carlson Woodward about that issue your father and I discussed. I terminated his employment, effective immediately."

Caroline hadn't thought she would feel guilty. But she did. Still, it would make Egan's job and her life easier without Carlson around. "Thank you," she told the manager.

"Don't thank me yet. Carlson was outraged. I think he'll probably try to sue you and your father."

"I can handle Carlson Woodward," she insisted.

Caroline thanked him again, clicked off the phone and waited until Egan finished his call. Judging from his responses, he was talking to Brody or Hayes because he mentioned the crime lab.

"What did the manager of the country club want?" Egan asked.

"He wanted to tell me that he fired Carlson."

A muscle went to work in Egan's jaw. "Did Carlson make threats about you?"

"Probably. But I doubt he said it to the manager's face. He'll need a reference to get another job so he likely held his tongue."

Egan shook his head. "References won't stop him from doing something petty to get back at you."

She remembered the story of Carlson's kidnapping the puppy. That sounded a few steps beyond petty.

"I'm more concerned about the killer right now." Caroline tipped her head to his cell phone, which he slipped back into his pocket. "Did you get news from the crime lab?"

"The crime scene analyst tested the lock they took

from your exterior bedroom door. It wasn't picked or tampered with. Whoever broke into your house and stole your dream journal used a key. It was a new key, one not used very often, if at all, because it left tiny shavings inside the lock."

That sent a chill through her. "And you want to know who has a copy of my key?"

He nodded. "Your father obviously has one because he threatened to use it. Who else?"

"Taylor." Someone she trusted with her life. But Caroline really hated to give the whereabouts of the final key she'd given out in case of an emergency. "Kenneth and Tammy Sutton have one."

Egan groaned. "Was it a new key?"

"Yes, a copy. And to the best of my knowledge, it's never been used."

"Hell," Egan cursed under his breath. He pulled out his phone and pressed in some numbers. "Brody," he said a moment later. "We need a search warrant. Kenneth Sutton has a copy of Caroline's house key. We need to have it checked for trace shavings. I want it compared to those that the crime lab found in the lock they removed from Caroline's bedroom door."

Caroline waited, her breath caught in her chest. "And then what?" she asked when Egan had finished the call. But she already knew the answer.

If the shavings were a match, then it likely meant that the person who wanted her dead was a man she'd known and trusted her entire life.

Kenneth Sutton.

Chapter Fifteen

Sitting on Caroline's pantry floor, Egan rubbed his hands over his face and checked his watch. Barely 8:00 p.m. This had already been one of the longest, and most eventful days he'd ever lived through. He hoped the eventfulness was over, but he wasn't holding out hope that the long day wouldn't turn into an equally long night.

Brody had just called to say he'd gotten the search warrant for Kenneth's house, and Hayes and he were on the way over to look for the copy of the key Caroline had given her neighbors in case of an emergency. Once they found it, the key would have to be taken to the lab, and those trace shavings would be compared to the ones found in the lock.

If it was a match, Kenneth and/or Tammy would be arrested. If they got lucky, one of them might even confess. And that meant this soon might be over.

"You should eat," Caroline insisted. She was sitting across from him, her legs stretched out in front of her, while she munched on Oreo cookies and bottled water.

It wasn't exactly great cuisine, and the pantry was stuffy, but it beat being in the kitchen with all those windows. As an extra precaution, Egan and Caroline had crawled from the foyer, and that would have to be her mode of travel throughout the house. Then tomorrow, if Kenneth or Tammy weren't in custody, he'd have to decide what to do about their living arrangements.

That included having Hayes swap places with Egan.

Egan wanted to stay with Caroline. And that was the problem. She was a major distraction to him. Especially now, with her bare feet, bare legs, rumpled clothes and his scent still all over her.

"Uh-oh," she mumbled. "I recognize that look. You're thinking about sex."

He lifted his eyebrow.

"About the sex between us that by now you believe shouldn't have happened," she clarified. Smiling, she leaned over and gave him a mouth-to-mouth kiss. "Don't worry. I have no expectations."

Well, she should. She deserved something better. And she sure as hell didn't deserve being stuck with a Texas Ranger bodyguard who couldn't stop thinking about her in a carnal sort of way. That kiss went through him like warmed whiskey, and he wanted her all over again.

Something that'd been happening all night.

"I'd like a hot bath," she said, putting her stash of snacks back on the shelf. She also put on her flip-flops. "How about you? Would you like to join me?"

Oh, man. That was some offer, and it was tempting. But if he got in that tub with a soapy, naked Caroline, they'd be all over each other again. Slick soap against slick body. Her breasts, and the rest of her, ready for the taking. That couldn't happen because he wanted to be alert and unaroused in case something went wrong.

"The security system will go off if someone breaks in," she reminded him.

True. He looked at her again, and the rationalizations started. Bad rationalization, about how he could have her one more time and that would somehow lessen his desire for her.

Yeah, right.

"Well?" she prompted.

Egan was on the verge of crawling down the hall with her to the bath, but his phone rang. Saved by the bell. But it wouldn't save him for long.

"Go ahead," he told her. "Keep the lights off, and stay away from the windows. I'll join you in a few minutes."

That earned him a chuckle and another kiss before she crawled away.

Egan motioned for her to go, cursed himself under his breath and answered the phone. "It's me, Taylor. Brody came by and got Caroline's house key, which she gave me months ago. He wouldn't say what was going on. Is everything okay with Caroline?"

"Caroline is…fine." It took him a moment to settle on that description, and Egan hated that it sounded sexual. Of course, he was thinking about sex so it probably came out in his tone. "We just need all the keys for some comparisons."

Egan left it at that. Best not to announce too many details of the investigation. But he did think of something else he wanted to question Taylor about. "Does your brother, Miles, have a gym bag with his initials on it?"

"Yes. I gave it to him for his last birthday. Why?"

Well, that was one mystery solved. "Have you seen it recently?"

"Funny you should mention it, I saw it just this morning. Miles had it with him when he dropped by on his way to the country club to play tennis."

Interesting. "Did he say anything about misplacing it a couple of days ago?"

"No. But that wouldn't surprise me if he had. Miles is always losing his things."

And in this case, Carlson simply could have been returning it. Nothing nefarious. No killer plans. "What about his shoes? Do you know if Miles owns a pair of tennis shoes called Razors? He would have bought them recently, in the past month probably, because they just came out."

"Let me check his credit card account. I pay his bills," Taylor added after a heavy sigh. He heard her make some key strokes on the computer. "I don't see any purchases at shoe stores or athletic stores. No online purchases, either."

"Could he have paid cash?" Egan asked.

"Miles doesn't have cash. If he bought them, he used the credit card, and it has a limit on how much he can spend."

Egan went in a different direction. "How about his friends—could one of them have purchased the shoes for him or given them to him as a gift?"

"Not likely. Let's just say my brother has tapped out all his friends when it comes to getting them to buy things for him. And despite Miles's penchant for spending money he doesn't have, he's never shoplifted."

So that left Egan with some big holes in the theory of Miles's possibly being the intruder. Of course, Miles could still be guilty, but right now Egan's money was on Kenneth.

If Kenneth had ordered his goon, Vincent Montoya, to kill Kimberly, then Kenneth could have killed Montoya and now simply be covering his tracks by trying to set up someone else, including Miles. And he could be trying to eliminate Caroline because he was afraid she'd remember something incriminating about that night.

Egan heard the slight click that indicated he had another call. "Thanks, Taylor. I'll talk to you soon." And he switched over to the other call.

"It's, uh, your father," the caller said.

Egan wasn't just surprised—he was shocked. He certainly hadn't expected to hear from him. "Look, if you're calling to put me in my social and economic place, forget it. I'm busy."

"I'm calling to save you some grief." He paused. "Egan, our kind doesn't mix with their kind."

That set his teeth on edge, even if it probably had some truth to it. "Is that fatherly advice?"

"No. I don't have a right to give you anything that's fatherly. I'm not apologizing for it, either. I did the best I could do."

"Did you?" Egan fired back.

His father cursed, but for once, it didn't seem to be aimed at Egan. "I was twenty years old when you were born. Just a kid myself. And then your mother…"

Egan waited. Holding his breath. "What about her?"

"She died, Egan." His father's voice cracked. "Her name was Mary, and she died right there in the hospital because the lowlife doctor at the charity hospital messed up something when he did the C-section to deliver you."

"Mary," Egan repeated. Yes, that was the name on his birth certificate, but until that moment it was the only thing he had known about her. That, and that she'd been barely nineteen. "I checked for a death certificate and didn't find one."

"Probably because her name wasn't Caldwell. It was Mary Buchanan. We never got around to getting married." His father paused. "I blamed you for her death."

Yes. Egan had always known he'd been blamed for something. Still, it hurt like hell to hear it confirmed. "Why didn't you just give me up for adoption?"

"Couldn't. Mary used her dying breath to tell me to take care of you. I told her I would. But I failed."

"Yeah. You did." Egan didn't intend to cut him any slack.

His father cleared his throat. "But you still turned out all right. You stood up to me tonight. You stood up to the Stallings, too."

No thanks to you, Egan wanted to say. But he couldn't. Because in an ironic sort of way, he could thank his father for his backbone. His father's neglect had taught Egan to stand up for himself because no one else ever had.

No one but Caroline.

"Do you love her?" his father asked.

Since the question seemed to come out of the blue, it took a moment to sink in. It took Egan another moment to realize he wasn't going to answer. And he wasn't going to think about it, either.

Hell, he wasn't even sure he knew what love was.

There was another clicking sound on his phone. Another call. He was obviously in big demand. Egan wasn't upset because it was a good time to end this chat with his father so he could have some time to process what the heck had just happened between them.

"I have to go," he told Walt. "Another call." He didn't wait for his father's response. Later, though, he might call him back and finish this conversation.

"It's Hayes," the caller said. "I'm at the Sutton house,

and Kenneth isn't here. He's supposedly downtown at a City Board meeting, but he's not answering his cell phone. Convenient, huh?"

Too convenient. But not being there wouldn't stop them from trying to learn the truth. "What about his wife?"

"Oh, she's here all right, shadowing my every move." And Egan could hear Tammy in the background. It sounded as if she was more than upset with Hayes's search. "When we got here, Tammy went to the kitchen drawer, where she says she kept Caroline's key. Guess what?"

Egan groaned. "It wasn't there."

"Bingo. Tammy says it's missing."

"Maybe because her husband has it," Egan quickly suggested.

"My thoughts exactly. Brody just left to try to find Kenneth at that meeting. I'll be here, probably all night, helping Ms. Sutton look for the key."

"Let me talk to him," Egan heard Tammy insist. A moment later, the woman came on the line. "Your Ranger friend here doesn't believe me. He thinks I know where the key is."

"And you don't?" Egan hoped his question conveyed his skepticism.

"I have no idea where it is. I think someone stole it," Tammy concluded.

"Who would do that?" Egan asked.

"Miles Landis." There wasn't a shred of hesitation in her voice. "He was here last week, asking for another loan. And I left him alone in the kitchen while I answered the phone. When I came back, he was rifling through the drawers."

Egan took a moment to process that. If she was telling the truth, and that was a big *if*, then it would explain how

Miles had gotten access to Caroline's. But if Miles had wanted a key, why hadn't he just taken it from his sister's place? That would have been far less risky than stealing from Tammy and Kenneth.

"Put Hayes back on the phone," Egan instructed.

"Yeah?" Hayes answered a moment later.

"Dust the kitchen drawers for prints."

"Will do."

Although they both knew it was a long shot. If Miles had indeed stolen the key, he'd probably wiped away his prints. Of course, sometimes criminals didn't do smart things, and Miles didn't appear to be that smart.

"I'll call Brody," Egan added. "Once he's located Kenneth and questioned him, the next person we should be interrogating is Miles."

"I agree. It might be a good idea if we got him off the street for a while. Or at least out of the neighborhood."

Yes. Miles Landis's name was popping up in all the wrong places, and Egan wanted to ask the man face-to-face if he was the one trying to kill Caroline.

WHILE EGAN WAS ON THE PHONE, Caroline crawled her way out of the kitchen, through her bedroom and onto the tiled bathroom floor. Just as Egan had instructed, she didn't turn on the lights. The room was definitely dark, the only illumination was the moonlight filtering through the crackled-texture thick glass blocks in the lone window at the far end of the room.

Fumbling around, she located the faucets and began to fill the tub. She considered adding bath oil, but she doubted Egan would want to smell like gardenias, and it was the only scent she had.

She caught a glimpse of herself in the mirror. Her face was there among the shadows. A troubled face, she noted. Despite her cavalier comment about having no expectations when it came to a relationship with Egan, she did have concerns. Not about him. But her.

Somewhere along the way, her feelings for him had crossed the line.

Her body wanted Egan. But her heart wanted him, too. And Caroline could see them having a relationship until the lust burned out. Which might take decades. Or it might end tomorrow. She wasn't sure how she would recover from that.

"Don't you dare fall this hard for him," she mumbled.

But realized it was already too late for that.

She closed her eyes and tried to deal with that in a logical sort of way. Unfortunately, no logic was going to change her mind.

Caroline turned to check the tub. She didn't hear footsteps exactly, because of the running water, but she sensed the sound and that she wasn't alone. She turned off the water and whirled around, expecting to see a crawling Egan making his way to her.

But it wasn't Egan.

Before she could even react, someone stepped out from the shadows, and a hand clamped hard over her mouth. He shoved the barrel of a pistol against her right temple.

"Oh, God," she mumbled beneath the intruder's hand. And she just kept repeating that because she didn't know what else to do.

The killer had obviously gotten in and had come for her. If she tried to call out, if she tried to scream, he'd put a bullet in her and would no doubt do the same to Egan when he came into the room.

"What do you want?" she asked, but her words were muffled.

He didn't answer. Instead, he dropped something on the floor. Something small that made a slight pinging sound when it landed on the tile.

Caroline could almost make out his reflection in the mirror. The man with the gun to her head.

But it wasn't till she heard his voice that she knew the truth.

"Ready to play a little kidnapping game, Caroline?" he whispered.

Chapter Sixteen

Egan cursed when he ended his call with Brody. Things just weren't going their way. Brody had located Kenneth at the meeting all right, but Kenneth was giving the same song and dance as his wife: that the key had obviously been stolen. If the pair stuck to that story, there wasn't much Egan could do, but he wasn't giving up.

He slipped his phone back into his pocket and got into a crouching position so he could make his way to Caroline's bathroom. Egan didn't even try to talk himself out of what he was going to do. Even if it was probably a mistake.

Too bad it didn't feel like a mistake.

But Caroline would be the one to pay for this so-called relationship. He'd seen the look in her father's eyes. The man thought Egan was scum.

Of course, Egan had seen the look in Caroline's eyes, too. And he'd heard her defend him. Still, in the back of his mind, he had to wonder if she knew what she was truly getting into with him.

He stood upright when he made it to her bathroom, and he picked through the darkness so he could find her.

Naked, hopefully. But he didn't see her there in the shadow-filled room.

"Caroline?" he called out softly.

Nothing.

Was this some kind of game? That's what Egan wanted to believe, but as a Ranger, he'd been trained to expect the worst. Besides, this wasn't a game Caroline would play.

He drew his weapon.

"Caroline?" His voice was louder now. His heart began to beat faster. Lots of really bad scenarios started to slam through his head.

Egan walked toward the tub to see if she was in the water, and his right boot landed on something small and hard. Maybe a shell casing. Keeping a vigilant watch around him, he reached down to retrieve what he'd stepped on.

It was something hard, but not a shell casing. More like a bit of molded plastic. A cracked button, maybe.

He held onto it and hurried to the tub. Caroline wasn't there. Thank God. She hadn't hit her head or drowned. That was the good news.

But the bad news was that she wasn't in the bathroom.

"Caroline?" he practically yelled.

Still no answer.

His instincts were to go racing through the house looking for her, but Egan held himself back. He had to think—not like her lover but like a Texas Ranger. If someone had broken in and was holding her at gunpoint, he had to figure out how to find her and get her free.

But was that what had happened?

Had someone broken in? Egan certainly hadn't heard anyone, and the security alarm hadn't gone off. Still, he knew that no security system was foolproof.

Keeping his gun drawn, he eased out of the bathroom and checked her bedroom. He tried to hurry. And he tried not to panic. That wouldn't do Caroline any good. But with each place he searched—under her bed, in the closet, in the sitting room—he had the sickening feeling that she was in grave danger.

Egan turned on the lamp in the sitting room to get a better look. She wasn't there. In case it was a clue of some kind, he checked the object he'd picked up from the bathroom floor.

He stared at it, a little blob of plastic painted gold. It took a moment to figure out exactly what it was.

"A golden Lab," he whispered. And he shook his head, not believing what he was seeing.

It'd been over twenty years since his pet had been stolen. Kidnapped. Locked in a storage shed.

By Carlson Woodward.

The impact of that slammed into Egan like a heavyweight's fist.

Hell.

Carlson had somehow broken in. He had Caroline. And he'd left the toy as a sick clue so that Egan would know his childhood nemesis was responsible. But responsible for what? Did Carlson intend to hurt Caroline?

Or worse—was Carlson the killer?

Egan whipped out his phone and called Hayes. "I need Brody and you here, *now.* I think Carlson kidnapped Caroline." He didn't wait for Hayes to respond. He shoved his phone back into his pocket and checked the closet of the sitting room in her bedroom suite. She wasn't there, either.

"Caroline!" he shouted.

Still nothing.

She had to be alive. She just had to be. Carlson wouldn't just kill her. No. He enjoyed the game too much for that. Was that what this was? A sick game?

Some movement caught his eye, and he spun in that direction. But it wasn't Caroline. It was the curtains on the window at the rear of the house. He bracketed his right wrist with his left hand and inched toward it.

The breeze didn't help. It stirred the white curtains, making them look like ghosts reaching out for him. Egan held his breath, and with each step, he listened and prayed.

He caught hold of the curtains. Snapped them back. And looked out into the backyard. The window screen had been removed and was lying on the ground.

Carlson had no doubt taken her out this way.

Egan heard the sound then. Well, *sounds* actually. Someone opened the garage door and started a car engine. He turned and raced toward the sound. Toward the garage.

But it was already too late.

Egan threw open the door, smelled the gas fumes and caught just a glimpse of Caroline's red Mustang as it sped away.

Cursing, and with his heart in his throat, Egan ran toward his Jeep, which he'd parked just off the side of the garage, extracting his keys as he ran. He rammed the key into the ignition. Turned it.

And nothing.

Damn! Carlson had obviously tampered with the engine. Egan didn't have time to figure out what was wrong. He had to go after Caroline. But how? He'd be useless on foot, and he couldn't wait for Hayes to arrive. That would mean precious moments lost.

He glanced around the garage, and he remembered the vintage Harley that Caroline had hidden away in the storage room. Egan raced toward it as if his life depended on it.

Because it did.

If he didn't get to Caroline in time, Carlson would kill her. And Egan would be dead inside if he wasn't able to save her.

"WHERE ARE YOU TAKING ME?" Caroline asked. She tried to make it sound like a demand, but even she could hear the fear in her voice.

Carlson had gone insane.

Thanks to the Cantara Hills streetlights, she could see his face. The muscles were tight. He was covered in oily sweat. His breathing was way too fast. And his eyes were wild and unfocused. Caroline didn't know if his present state was drug-induced or if this was a side of him that he'd kept hidden away, only allowing it to break free so he could kidnap her at gunpoint.

Driving too fast and steering with one shaky hand, Carlson made a sharp turn, not out of the neighborhood but toward the part of it that had yet to be developed. Caroline hiked there sometimes, and it was rugged, with dense trees and shrubs littered with limestone bluffs. Some low. And some, like the one they were approaching, high. This one was at least thirty feet up and rimmed the narrow two-lane road for several miles.

Carlson kept the gun gripped in his right hand, and it was pointed right at her heart. She could try to knock the gun away, but it would be a huge risk, especially at the speed he was going. If he didn't shoot her, there would certainly be an accident, and neither of them would survive if the car plunged off the limestone bluff.

Since he hadn't answered any of her questions so far, Caroline took a different approach. She had to get him talking so that she could maybe distract him. "How did you get past the security system at my house?"

"I followed your parents." His voice was soft, which was more unsettling than a shout would have been. That voice was also an alarming contrast to the rest of his appearance and body language. "Put on your seat belt," he insisted. "I don't want you trying to jump from the car."

Of course not. Caroline stretched the belt across her lap and shoulder, but she didn't fasten it.

"I need to hear the click, Caroline," he demanded. "Do it. Because I don't want to have to shoot you in the car."

But he would.

His tone made that very clear.

Caroline fastened the seat belt and prayed she'd get an opportunity to escape.

"When you turned off your security system to let your parents in your house, that's when I broke the latch on your sitting room window," he calmly explained. "All of you were talking so loud, you didn't even hear me. Then I climbed in and hid. I figured you'd eventually come back there to that part of the house."

Oh, mercy. That meant Carlson had been inside for an hour or more. Lurking. Waiting. It made her skin crawl.

And unfortunately, his plan had worked.

He'd waited, and now he had her. But why? Did he really intend to kill her?

"Where are you taking me?" she repeated.

"We're going to play a game." His voice was even softer now. Practically a whisper. "With Egan."

That chilled her to the bone, and Caroline glanced behind them to see if Egan was there. He wasn't.

But he soon would be.

Somehow, someway, Egan would find her. Carlson knew that as well, and he was probably going to set some kind of a trap so he could kill them both or make Egan watch while he killed her.

"This doesn't have anything to do with the murders?" She wanted to know.

"Why would it? Caroline, this is between me and you. Oh, and of course, Egan."

Of course. She'd known that Carlson disliked both Egan and her, but she'd obviously underestimated just how far he'd go. "If you want revenge for getting fired, then leave Egan out of this."

He smiled. "What, and have him miss all the fun? He's missed too much fun in his life."

Anger began to replace her fear. This sick SOB actually planned to use her and his being fired from his job to get back at Egan. "This isn't fun, and it wasn't fun when you kidnapped Egan's golden Lab puppy twenty years ago. It's sick, Carlson. *You're* sick. You need help."

He took his eyes off the road and glared at her. Not an ordinary glare. She saw nothing but savageness in those feral eyes.

With his jaw muscles working as if they'd declared war on each other, he stomped on the accelerator, right before he made the final turn that would lead them to the peak of the bluff. Because she was watching him so closely, she saw the surprised look. For just a split second.

Before he grabbed the steering wheel with both hands.

Caroline knew this was her chance. Maybe her only chance. She had to escape.

She reached for the handle of the door, but reaching for it was as far as she got. The car went into a sharp skid. Carlson grappled with the steering wheel and slammed on the brakes. It didn't help.

The Mustang plowed right into a tree.

Air bags burst out from the dash, and hers slammed into her face. Her father had insisted that she add the bags after she had bought the vintage vehicle. Good thing, too. Because it only took Caroline a few seconds to realize the air bag had probably saved her life.

It'd saved Carlson's life, too.

He cursed, and she followed his gaze to the rearview mirror. Caroline heard the sound, too. A motorcycle. Her Harley. She glanced back and spotted Egan riding straight up the hill toward them.

"Let's go," Carlson ordered.

He got her out of the seat belt, and with a death grip on her arm, he practically dragged her from the car. If he had even minor injuries, he didn't show it. Carlson maneuvered her into the thick trees that lipped the bluff, and he started running with her in tow.

Caroline stumbled. Partly from the flip-flops she was wearing and partly because she wanted to slow him down. It didn't work. Carlson simply wrenched her arm until she was back in a standing position, and they ran again.

Behind them, she heard Egan kill the engine on the Harley. She also heard his running footsteps. He was coming after her.

Carlson obviously realized that, too.

Because he stopped and dragged her in front of him, putting her between Egan and him.

Caroline got just a glimpse of Egan.

As Carlson fired a shot at him.

Chapter Seventeen

Egan dove behind a scraggly mesquite oak.

Barely in time.

The bullet from Carlson's gun flew past him and slammed into a limestone outcropping to his right. Too close. The mesquite wouldn't be much protection if Carlson continued to fire at him. Besides, he couldn't stay put and try to keep himself out of harm's way.

He had to get to Caroline.

With a firm grip on his service pistol, Egan glanced out to assess the situation. He didn't like what he saw. Carlson had his arm curved around Caroline's throat, and he had the gun pointed at her head. There was no way he could get off a safe shot to take Carlson out because the man was literally using Caroline as a human shield.

That in itself was enough to make Egan's pulse pound out of control, but the gun and Carlson weren't the only danger. Nature wasn't on their side, either. Carlson was standing in the moonlight just a few feet from the edge of a jagged limestone bluff. Egan knew from experience that the limestone was often unstable and could give way. If that happened…

Well, he refused to think beyond that.

His only goal was to save Caroline.

Egan peered out and met her gaze. For only a second. It was all he could handle, or it would distract him at a time when he needed no more distractions. But he couldn't completely dismiss that look he saw on Caroline's face. Not fear. Not even a hint of it. And that cut him to the bone. Because he knew it cost more to hide the fear than to show it.

"You aren't doing yourself any favors," Egan told Carlson. "Surrender your weapon, and you won't be hurt. You've got my word on that." He kept his voice calm, void of any emotion. Like the look on Caroline's face, it was a well-concealed lie. Beneath the badge and the gun, there was a storm of emotions. He didn't intend to let Caroline die.

"Surrender my weapon?" Carlson repeated. He gave a hollow laugh and backed up a step, moving himself closer to that lethal edge of the bluff.

"Carlson, you're going to fall. Look behind you. The fall will kill you. You really want to die at the bottom at that bluff?"

Carlson didn't take the bait. He didn't look away and divert his attention from Caroline. "Death is death," he concluded. "We all have to go sometime."

Egan cursed. "What the hell happened to you to make you do this?"

He expected Carlson to launch into a tirade about how getting fired had humiliated him, about how all that garbage during their childhoods had affected him. But Carlson only shook his head and looked at the gun he held as if seeing it for the first time.

"Are you wasted on something?" Egan asked. If so, that made this situation even more dangerous. It was hard to bargain with someone whose mind was in a drug-hazed cloud. Strange, though, Egan had heard no rumors or reports that Carlson was a user.

Carlson didn't respond to Egan's question, but his expression changed. The cockiness evaporated, and he kept shaking his head as if trying to clear it. What he didn't do was let go of Caroline.

And he kept the gun pointed right at her.

Egan eased out several inches from the tree so he'd be in a better position to get off a shot. If the opportunity arose. If it didn't, then he'd have to create one.

"Don't come any closer," Carlson warned.

He moved.

Not backward, thank God. But to the side. Toward a dense cluster of cedars and underbrush. Beyond that was a wooded area and perhaps even an escape route. Egan wasn't familiar with the area, but he knew there were old ranching trails and dirt roads that snaked around the property.

Hopefully, Carlson didn't have another vehicle stashed out there somewhere.

Caroline's expression didn't change, but she no doubt knew what this scum was capable of doing. Her life wouldn't be worth a dime if he somehow managed to get away from Egan. Carlson would just take her to a secondary crime scene.

"Tell me what it'll take to get you to release her," Egan bargained. "You've got to give me something to bargain with here." He hoped it would stop Carlson from moving.

It didn't.

Carlson just kept inching toward those cedars that would conceal him. "Nothing will make me release her."

"He's playing the kidnapping game," Caroline said. "He didn't hurt the puppy twenty years ago. I don't think he'll hurt me, either."

Carlson stopped and made direct eye contact with Egan. "I made a mistake that day. I should have hurt that damn dog and set you up to take the blame. They would have sent you somewhere. Maybe juvenile hall so I wouldn't have to live on the same street with you."

It sickened Egan to hear Carlson speak so casually about doing harm to an animal. And it made him think of something he should have already asked. He wanted a confession. "Did you hire Montoya to kill Kimberly McQuade and the others?"

The corner of Carlson's mouth lifted into an uneasy smile. "No."

Egan didn't believe him, even if Carlson seemed adamant about it. "Then if you're not a killer, why start now?"

"Because Caroline deserves to die. And you deserve to watch her die." Carlson tightened his arm around her throat, and he shoved the gun even harder against her temple.

Caroline dug in her heels when he tried to drag her closer to those cedars. "Okay. I'm not saying this because I think I'm going to die. I won't. But just in case, I want you to know this isn't your fault. And I have no regrets about what happened between us."

It was pure bravado. Egan could hear the fear in her voice. She was trying to say goodbye.

And Egan wasn't going to let her.

"Carlson, I'll trade places with Caroline," Egan insisted. "It's me you really want to kill anyway."

He blinked away the sweat that was sliding down his face. "Oh, I want both of you dead. I just want her to be first so you have to watch."

Carlson stood there. Staring at Egan. His hands were shaking now. And he dragged his tongue over his bottom lip. For just a moment, Egan thought Carlson might change his mind. He prayed that whatever drug was clouding his mind the effects were dissipating and Carlson was coming to his senses.

Egan inched out from the tree. He kept his gun aimed. Just in case he could get a clean shot. But that wasn't his first course of action. He wanted to talk Carlson into surrendering his weapon. And Caroline.

"Let's talk," Egan calmly suggested. He got to his feet. Stood. And stared Carlson down.

Carlson's mouth opened slightly. As if he were about to say something. But he didn't utter a word. Neither did Egan. Before he could say a thing, Carlson shifted his gun. Away from Caroline.

Carlson fired.

And the pain exploded through Egan as the bullet hit him.

CAROLINE HEARD HERSELF scream.

But the sound was muffled by the deafening blast of the shot.

Everything slowed to a crawl and felt thick and syrupy. Maybe because her mind couldn't absorb the sheer horror of what she was witnessing.

Egan had been shot.

Caroline's breath vanished. Her heart kicked against

her chest. In front of her, Egan dove back to the cover of the tree. But it was too late.

The blood. God, the blood. She'd seen it spattered across the front of his shirt.

"Egan!" she called out.

Caroline fought to get loose from Carlson so she could go to him. Egan needed help. But Carlson held on to her, even tightening his grip, and he growled some kind of warning in her ear. She didn't care about warnings or what this SOB might do to her.

She had to get to Egan.

"Keep fighting me, and I'll finish him off right now," Carlson added.

Caroline clearly heard that. The words made it into her adrenaline-spiked, fight-mode brain. And because Carlson would carry through on that threat, she stopped struggling. For a moment, anyway, so that she could figure out what to do.

Begging was the easiest option. "Please, Carlson, let me help him."

Carlson didn't react to her plea. He started to move again, dragging her in the direction of the dense cedars.

Caroline tried to hold her ground, but her shoes didn't cooperate. The jeweled flip-flops obviously weren't meant to navigate rugged terrain, and she couldn't keep her footing. She practically fell face-first into the cover of those trees and shrubs.

She looked back, trying to get a glimpse of Egan. He was still there, behind the mesquite. And he was moving. Well, he was glancing at them. But she couldn't tell if he was alert or if he was losing consciousness. He was certainly losing blood, and he needed an ambulance.

And Carlson was responsible for this.

Along with the adrenaline, Caroline felt the anger ripple through her. The enraged emotion took over, and she ignored Carlson's warnings, drew back her elbow and jammed him hard in his belly.

Carlson staggered back. Just a step. Not enough to get him to release the grip he had on her, though.

"Try that again, and you die." He called her a name. Not a flattering one, either, and gave her another shove.

Caroline didn't give up. She couldn't. Egan's life was at stake. This time, she went for the gun. She turned, using her body to ram into him, and in the same motion, she tried to grab the gun. She wasn't quite successful, but she did manage to latch on to his right wrist. She dug her nails into his skin, drawing blood.

"Caroline, don't!" Egan shouted.

From the corner of her eye, she saw Egan come out from the cover of the tree. Carlson obviously saw him, too, because even though she still had a grip on his wrist, he managed to turn the gun in Egan's direction.

Carlson's sheer strength stunned her. He threw off her grip as if she were a gnat, and he fired another shot.

At Egan.

Egan dropped to the ground again, and the bullet kicked up some dirt and rocks just behind him. He took aim at Carlson, but he didn't shoot. Because of her. Carlson moved behind her again, preventing Egan from returning fire.

"How badly are you hurt?" she called out to Egan.

"I'll live," was his answer. But he sounded weak, and in that brief glimpse of him, she'd seen the blood that now covered the right shoulder and sleeve of his shirt.

It felt as if someone had clamped a fist around her heart.

She'd known Egan was important to her. She'd known she cared about him. But she hadn't known how much.

Until that moment.

Caroline blinked back the tears that tried to form in her eyes. It wasn't exactly an ideal moment to realize that she was in love with him.

Carlson hooked his forearm around her neck and got her moving again—toward those cedars. She couldn't go there. It would give Carlson the perfect cover to dodge any gunfire from Egan. And it would give Carlson the perfect place to kill her. Then he would lie in wait so he could ambush Egan when he came after her.

Caroline had no doubts whatsoever about that. Which meant she had nothing to lose. She had to get away now if she stood any chance of getting Egan help in time.

She dropped down, using her weight to propel herself toward the ground. Egan reacted. He came out from the tree and took aim.

Carlson's grip slipped from her neck.

That was her opportunity. And she took it. Caroline started to run.

She'd made it only a few steps before Carlson fired his gun.

EGAN IGNORED THE PAIN that speared through his arm and shoulder, and he got to his feet. He didn't have time to take aim at Carlson before the man tackled Caroline. He could only watch as the two plummeted to the ground, and Carlson scrambled into the cedars with her.

Carlson had her—again.

Caroline hadn't been able to escape.

Hell. It'd taken ten years off his life when he'd seen

Carlson fire that shot at her. But she hadn't been hit. Thank God. Egan was sure of that. The bullet had landed against a limestone boulder. He'd seen the spray of pellets and dust. Close. But not close enough.

They'd gotten lucky.

That luck might not continue.

"Caroline?" Egan yelled.

"Stay back, Egan," Carlson warned. His voice was frantic now, and he sounded out of breath from the exertion of the struggle with Caroline.

"Is Caroline all right?" Egan had to know. It was a battle just to stand there, but if he went charging into the cedars, Carlson would likely shoot her first.

"For now," Carlson answered.

Good. That was a start. "Carlson, this has to end. You have to let her go."

"So you've said. But we haven't played the game yet."

Egan groaned and clamped his left hand over his shoulder when he felt the flow of blood increase. "There's no game to play," Egan shouted. "Just release her."

Carlson didn't say anything for several seconds. "You won't win this time, Egan. I swear. You won't win."

The words chilled him to the bone.

Egan stood there. Listening. Praying. It was hard to hear anything with his heartbeat drumming in his ears, but he was sure he didn't hear the sirens or Hayes. With his attention and his weapon aimed on those cedars, he took out his phone.

Hayes answered on the first ring. "Where the hell are you, Egan?"

"Cantara Hills. Top of the bluff. You'll see Caroline's wrecked Mustang." Egan had to force himself to steady his breathing. And hell, he was getting dizzy. "Carlson took her hostage, and he shot me."

Hayes cursed. "How bad?"

"It hurts worse than it is." Egan hoped.

"I'm on the way, and I'll call an ambulance."

Good. Because he would need one. He hoped he'd be the only one who did. Egan ended the call and put away his phone so he'd have both hands to continue this battle.

"Caroline?" Egan shouted.

She didn't answer.

But he did hear something.

Something that put Egan's stomach in a hard knot. The sound of footsteps. Hurried ones.

Carlson was on the move with her. That was good news. In a way. It meant he hadn't tried to kill her. Instead, he'd likely continued what he considered to be a game. Some game. Caroline and he were fighting for their lives.

Egan couldn't stay put, and he couldn't wait for help from Hayes. It might be too late. He left the meager cover of the tree and raced in the direction of those footsteps. With his hand still pressed over his wound, he made his way through the cedars.

They weren't there.

But there were signs of a struggle. Snapped tree branches and swirls of shoe prints on the moonlit ground. A red fake gem from Caroline's shoes sparkled amid the crushed limestone.

There was a small clearing ahead of him, and just beyond that, more trees. He paused to get his bearings and to figure out the best way to approach the area.

Then a shot tore through the hill country.

A single bullet. Followed by no sounds. No screams. No shouts for help. *Hell.* Caroline might be hurt. Or worse.

Egan didn't stop, although he knew in the back of his mind that Carlson could be waiting in those trees to ambush him. He tore through the clearing, ignoring the pain and the dizziness. He had to get to her.

He raced into the trees, bashing aside the low-hanging branches. Egan had to hurdle over a large fallen oak, and he cursed when the landing caused pain to stab through him. Still, he didn't slow down. He headed straight for the moonlight that was threading its way through the trees.

And he came out the other side.

Still no sign of Caroline. No sign of blood, either.

Egan barreled over a six-foot-high uneven limestone outcropping.

And practically skidded to a stop.

Dead center in front of him was Caroline and Carlson. He still had her in a death grip. Arm around her throat. A gun to her head.

She was alive.

And other than some scrapes to her knees, she appeared to be unharmed.

Egan was more than thankful for that but not for what else he saw. There was another limestone bluff. Higher than the first one he'd encounter.

That was where Carlson had Caroline.

On the edge of it.

The heels of Carlson's shoes weren't even on the ground. With the grip he had on Caroline, if Carlson fell, then she would, too.

"Carlson, you don't want to do this," Egan bargained.

But he apparently did want to do this. Carlson's expression was flat now, and his skin had turned pale. Whatever drug he was on, it was playing havoc with his body and his mind. The man was obviously insane.

"I'm tired of this game," Carlson mumbled. He shook his head and took aim at Egan. "It's time for it to end."

Egan walked a step closer. "It doesn't have to be this way." Maybe he could keep Carlson talking until Hayes arrived.

Caroline's gaze met Egan's. Carlson might be ready to end this, but she wasn't. There was resolve in her eyes. And concern. She kept glancing at his blood-soaked shirt.

"I'm okay," he lied to her.

"No, you're not." She angled her eyes back at Carlson. "Please let me call for an ambulance. For both of you. You need help, too."

"She's right," Egan added. "Whatever drug you took has messed with your mind."

"I didn't take a drug." And Carlson was resolute about it. For a second or two, anyway. Then he shook his head again. "Did I? I don't remember taking anything."

"That's why you need to put down the gun and come away from the bluff. The drug will wear off, and you'll know then that you made the right decision."

Carlson seemed to think about that. He stared at Egan. Glanced at Caroline. Before looking at his gun. It finally seemed to be registering that what he was doing was stupid and reckless.

His attention landed on Egan again. Specifically, at the fast-spreading blood pool on his shirt. Hopefully, Carlson wouldn't notice that Egan was having trouble seeing. The dizziness was making everything flash in and out of focus.

"If I put down my gun," Carlson said, "I'll go to jail

for attempted murder of a Texas Ranger. If you don't kill me first, that is."

Carlson put the gun back to Caroline's head. And the corner of his mouth lifted into a smile. "I might as well win part of this game. I can take her away from you, Egan. I can make you have to live with seeing her die."

The anger went bone-deep inside Egan, and he went a step closer.

Carlson leaned back. Nearly tipping himself off-balance. And he laughed. It was as sick as that stupid grin on his face.

"Say goodbye to him, Caroline," Carlson insisted.

Her bottom lip quivered a little before she hiked up her chin. "I love you."

Egan couldn't have possibly been more stunned if she'd shot him. He didn't question it, nor did he take the time to consider if it was the adrenaline talking. He made his decision about what to do and then said a quick prayer that Caroline would do what was necessary to survive.

Egan lifted his gun. Aimed it.

At Carlson.

Maybe the dizziness would wait until he finished this.

"No!" Caroline yelled. Her voice echoed through the canyon below. It echoed in his head.

"Move!" Egan shouted to her.

Carlson reacted. He whipped the gun from her so he could aim it at Egan. Caroline did exactly what Egan wanted her to do. In the chaos of the moment and the re-shifting, she slung both arms at Carlson's body. Her elbows battered him. Then, she dropped to the ground.

Carlson fired.

Egan didn't even take the time to feel if he'd been hit again. He did what he was trained to do. He took aim.

And fired.

Two shots. A double tap of gunfire. Shots meant to kill. The gun blasts ripped through the air, drowning out everything else.

The bullets went where Egan had intended them to go. Straight into Carlson's heart.

Carlson went stiff, his hands dropping to his sides. His gun clattered to the ground. There was almost no life left him, but he met Egan eye-to-eye. For just a split-second, Egan saw the shock. The realization of what had just happened.

Maybe even the regret.

Egan watched as Carlson's eyelids closed, and he dropped backward over the ledge. Seconds later, he heard the thud. Saw Caroline scrambling to get to him. But the dizziness took over. And Egan felt himself fall to the ground.

The last thing he heard was Caroline screaming his name.

Chapter Eighteen

Egan struggled to open his eyes. The fight was still with him, and the images of Carlson ripped through his head. He automatically reached for his gun.

Which wasn't there.

But the pain was.

Cursing, he forced himself to focus and realized he wasn't in the woods near Cantara Hills. He was in the hospital with an IV in the back of his right hand and with his left shoulder and arm bandaged. Machines beeped around him.

"Carlson shot me," he mumbled. "I shot him."

"Yes," he heard someone say. He knew that voice. It was Caroline. "But you're alive, and you're going to make a full recovery. The bullet went clean through and didn't do nearly as much damage as it could have."

Wincing as he moved his shoulder, Egan turned slightly and spotted her. Not that he had to look far. Caroline was there, right next to his bed. Behind her, looming over her, stood Brody and Hayes. Both were staring down at him and had plenty of concern on their somber faces.

Caroline looked concerned, too.

And she had blood on her top.

Adrenaline shot through him. *Hell*. She'd been hurt. Carlson had hurt her. Egan tried to get up so he could make sure she was okay.

Caroline stopped him. She gently but firmly put her hand on his uninjured shoulder and eased him back onto the bed. She followed his gaze and shook her head. "No. I wasn't injured. This is your blood."

His blood. Egan had to give that some thought, but yes, that made sense. "Right," he mumbled.

"You left a lot of your blood in the woods, in the ambulance and on Caroline," Hayes informed him. "It could have been more if Caroline hadn't put pressure on the gunshot wound. I don't guess it occurred to you to wait until I got there before you went after Carlson?"

Egan ignored the mandatory scolding, and his gaze connected with Brody's. He got no such scolding from him, because Brody likely understood why Egan had done what he did. If Brody's fiancé, Victoria, had been Carlson's hostage, Brody wouldn't have waited for backup, either.

"Carlson is dead," Brody explained.

Yeah. Egan knew that. No one could have survived that fall from the bluff. "Make sure the coroner does a tox screen. Carlson was high on something."

Brody nodded. "Caroline told us." He paused. "She also told us that Carlson said he was playing some kidnapping game."

Egan remembered that as well, and it made him sick to his stomach. "We'll have to connect Carlson to Vincent Montoya," Egan said, thinking out loud. "Carlson probably paid him, or blackmailed him, to go after Kimberly the night of the hit-and-run."

Which meant Carlson had tried to kill Caroline that night, too. But why? Maybe because Carlson thought when Caroline's memory fully returned that she would be able to link him to Montoya and the hit-and-run? Maybe this was Carlson's way of tying up potential loose ends that could send him to prison and even get him the death penalty.

Was that it?

But Carlson had also tried to kill Egan. Of course, there was bad blood between them. Carlson hated him, and he probably didn't mind adding Egan to his kill-list so that he could stop him from learning the truth and get some revenge for all the petty things that'd happened between them as kids. Carlson had probably spent a long time stewing over that bad blood, and along with the help of some kind of drug, he'd finally got the *courage* to do something.

Thank God he hadn't succeeded.

"*We'll* connect Carlson to Montoya," Hayes insisted. He was adamant about it, too. "As in Brody and I will do that. You're looking at a minimum of two days here in San Antonio General and at least two weeks of time off after that. Those are orders from the captain."

Egan was already shaking his head before Hayes finished. "The case—"

"Will be taken care of," Brody finished. "Hayes and I will finish off things."

Egan looked at Caroline to back him up, but she only folded her arms over her chest and gave him a flat stare. "I watched you nearly die, and I'm wearing a pint of your blood. If you think I'm going to give you my blessing to go straight back to work, then you're wrong."

And then she did something else that surprised him.

Caroline leaned over and kissed him.

Not a peck, either. A real kiss. Slow. Deep. Long. Under different circumstances, he would have thought it was foreplay, but when she pulled back, he saw the tears in her eyes.

She quickly blinked them away. "Seeing you shot scared me." Simply explained, but he could see the intensity of her feelings. This had shaken her to the core.

Egan understood that. Seeing Carlson's gun at her head had shaken him, too.

"You owe me," Caroline added.

He wasn't in so much pain that he couldn't feel a little outraged, and confused, by that. "Excuse me?"

"Because you scared me so much, you owe me your cooperation. You're going to take that time off, and you're going to get well."

He didn't argue, mainly because her tears started to return. And with Carlson out of the picture, time off didn't sound so bad.

Brody cleared his throat. "We'll be going. Caroline's right—heal. Get better. And don't worry about the case. There are just a few loose ends that need to be tied up. That's all."

Yes. A killer was dead. And Caroline was no longer in danger. All in all, that was worth the bullet hole he had in his shoulder.

Brody nodded a goodbye. Hayes punched him on his good shoulder. "I'm leaving Caroline some rope in case she has to tie you up," Hayes joked.

Caroline waited until they'd left before she winked at Egan. "You think you'd like being tied up?" She smiled, and it was dazzling despite the fatigue and worry he could see in her eyes.

"Tied up by you?" Egan caught her arm and eased her down beside him. "How could I say no to a woman with a Harley, a rope and some apparently really raunchy ideas?"

He pulled her closer and kissed her this time. The taste of her went right through him, and he could have sworn that it lessened the pain.

She pulled back, licked the taste of him from her lips. "Your father called a couple of minutes before you woke up."

Egan had to repeat it to himself to make sure he'd heard her correctly. "My father?"

"Yes, he sounded worried."

Egan was about to dismiss it. But he didn't. Maybe that phone call in the pantry had really been the start of some fence mending. Egan wasn't sure that was possible, but after being given a second chance at life, he wasn't about to close any doors just yet.

"I asked Hayes, and he said you have a great little house in Austin. Maybe I could stay there with you while you're recovering?" Caroline asked.

He thought of his house and suddenly didn't feel so warm and fuzzy. And he rethought that door closing part. "It's a fixer-upper."

"Sounds perfect."

He shook his head. "It's not exactly your style."

"Sounds perfect," she repeated. The smile returned. "You've got to revise this notion you have of me, Egan, that I have to live in luxury. I own a Harley, remember? It's my prize possession, not that Victorian house my parents bought me."

Yes. He was beginning to see that. Cool and expensive on the outside. But inside, Caroline Stallings was, well, hot. And she was his kind of woman.

Now, the question was—what was he going to do about it?

He could keep things status quo. Give them time to build a relationship and be absolutely certain that they were right for each other. It was what he would usually do when faced with a complex decision.

Approach with caution.

Stay guarded.

Then walk away before things could develop into something deeper.

But the idea of walking away from Caroline actually made his heart ache.

And what he felt for her was already something deeper.

"Uh-oh," she mumbled. "You're thinking about breaking up with me."

"No." He said it quickly to get it out of the way. Breaking up was the last thing he wanted to do with her.

Smiling, she moved closer, until her mouth was hovering over his. "Well, you can't do *that* with me right now. But after you've recovered…" She let her words linger between them, and it fueled a fantasy or two.

He whispered one of those fantasies to her. It involved her naked and on her Harley. Actually, on his lap while on the Harley.

She moved her mouth against his ear. "You're a wild child, Egan Caldwell." She kissed his earlobe. Laughed. "I love that about you."

Then she stiffened and got that deer-caught-in-the-headlights look. Probably because she thought that would be his sign to start building a wall between them. The leave 'em time.

But Egan had something else in mind.

It was a risk. A Texas-sized one. Still, it was time he took a risk like that.

He held her chin and forced eye contact, something she was suddenly avoiding. "What would your parents say if I were to ask you to marry me?"

She blinked. Then, stared at him. "W-hat?"

His heart started to pound, and he wondered if that Texas-sized risk was about to be a Texas-sized mistake. "What if I asked you to marry me?" he paraphrased. "What would your parents say?"

And he held his breath.

Caroline seemed to have a little trouble breathing as well. "They wouldn't like it. Well, not at first, but I think after they got to know you, they would warm up to the idea. Why?" She swallowed hard. "Was that a proposal?"

He skimmed his thumb over her bottom lip. "You're my type, you know that?"

"Really? You're my type, too," she said quickly. "Now, back to the other thing. Was that an honest-to-goodness marriage proposal?"

Egan tried to look self-assured and was certain he failed. "What if it was, hypothetically speaking?"

She eyed him with skepticism. "Hypothetically speaking—then I'd have to say that I'd marry you in a heartbeat."

"A heartbeat?" *Okay.* That sounded good. To him. But he had to wonder. "You could have anyone you want."

"Good." Her voice was hardly more than a whisper, but she cleared her throat to give it some sound. "Because I want you." She paused and fondled her locket. "Does that mean I can have you?"

Did it? Egan thought he'd better clarify things first. "Life with me wouldn't be easy. I'm the surly one, remember?"

She didn't disagree. "Okay."

"And I work long hours."

Caroline pressed her fingers over his mouth. Frowned. "Are you trying to talk me out of my hypothetical yes that I'd marry you in a heartbeat?"

He eased her fingers away after he kissed them. "I'm just trying to make you understand that I'm no prize."

A sigh left her mouth, and before he could guess what was coming, she kissed him, Caroline-style. "I." She kissed him again. "Love." Another kiss. "You."

That was the answer he was looking for, but it still took him several moments to let it sink in. It sank in very well. "So, the question is no longer hypothetical. Caroline Stallings, will you marry me?"

"In less than a heartbeat." She smiled against his mouth. He could almost taste that smile, and he could feel her happiness.

Well, for a couple of seconds, anyway.

She pulled back slightly so they were eye-to-eye. "Why do you want to marry me?"

Oh, man. There it was. The question he'd tiptoed around for the past five minutes. And his entire life.

"I know it's not for my money," she said when he didn't answer. "Or my house." She lifted her shoulder and gave him a teasing look that he was becoming familiar with.

She was going to give him an out.

She wasn't going to make him say it.

"But it could be because we have great sex," she continued. She snapped her fingers. "I got it. You want to marry me because of my 1951 Panhead Harley Chopper."

"No." He could do this. He wasn't a wimp. But facing down bad guys seemed easy compared to this.

He took a dose of courage by sliding his hand around the back of her neck and hauling her to him so he could kiss her. He didn't stop until they both had to gasp for air.

"I'm not marrying you for the money, the house or the Harley," he let her know. Clarifying that was important.

And it was something he'd waited his life to say.

"Caroline, I'm marrying you for one reason. Well, two, actually. I want to marry you because I want to spend the rest of my life with you."

Those beautiful eyes shimmered with tears, and they were definitely of the happy variety. "And the other reason?" Her voice was all breath and hope.

Egan was filled the same hope. "Because I love you."

He pulled her into arms and showed her just how much.

* * * * *

THE SILVER STAR OF TEXAS:
CANTARA HILLS INVESTIGATION
comes to an explosive conclusion next month when
award-winning author Rita Herron presents
BENEATH THE BADGE,
only from Harlequin Intrigue!

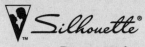

Romantic
SUSPENSE

Sparked by Danger,
Fueled by Passion.

Cindy Dees
Killer Affair

Seduction in the sand…and a killer on the beach.

Can-do girl Madeline Crummby is off to a remote
Fijian island to review an exclusive resort, and she hires
Tom Laruso, a burned-out bodyguard, to fly her there
in spite of an approaching hurricane. When their plane
crashes, they are trapped on an island with a serial killer
who stalks overaffectionate couples. When their false
attempts to lure out the killer turn all too real, Tom and
Madeline must risk their lives and their hearts….

**Look for the third installment
of this thrilling miniseries,
available August 2008
wherever books are sold.**

HARLEQUIN

More Than Words

"The more I see, the more I feel the need."

—Aviva Presser, real-life heroine

Aviva Presser is a Harlequin More Than Words
award winner and the founder of Bears Without Borders.

Discover your inner heroine!

MTW07API

HARLEQUIN

More Than Words

"Aviva gives the best bear hugs!"

—**Jennifer Archer,** author

*Jennifer wrote "Hannah's Hugs," inspired by Aviva Presser, founder of **Bears Without Borders**, a nonprofit organization dedicated to delivering the comfort and love of a teddy bear to severely ill and orphaned children worldwide.*

Look for "*Hannah's Hugs*" in
More Than Words, Vol. 4,
available in April 2008 at eHarlequin.com
or wherever books are sold.

SUPPORTING CAUSES OF CONCERN TO WOMEN **HARLEQUIN**
WWW.HARLEQUINMORETHANWORDS.COM

MTW07AP2

REQUEST YOUR FREE BOOKS!

2 FREE NOVELS
PLUS 2
FREE GIFTS!

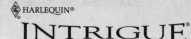

HARLEQUIN®

INTRIGUE®

Breathtaking Romantic Suspense

YES! Please send me 2 FREE Harlequin Intrigue® novels and my 2 FREE gifts (gifts are worth about $10). After receiving them, if I don't wish to receive any more books, I can return the shipping statement marked "cancel." If I don't cancel, I will receive 6 brand-new novels every month and be billed just $4.24 per book in the U.S. or $4.99 per book in Canada, plus 25¢ shipping and handling per book and applicable taxes, if any*. That's a savings of close to 15% off the cover price! I understand that accepting the 2 free books and gifts places me under no obligation to buy anything. I can always return a shipment and cancel at any time. Even if I never buy another book from Harlequin, the two free books and gifts are mine to keep forever.

182 HDN EEZ7 382 HDN EEZK

Name	(PLEASE PRINT)	
Address		Apt. #
City	State/Prov.	Zip/Postal Code

Signature (if under 18, a parent or guardian must sign)

Mail to the **Harlequin Reader Service:**
IN U.S.A.: P.O. Box 1867, Buffalo, NY 14240-1867
IN CANADA: P.O. Box 609, Fort Erie, Ontario L2A 5X3

Not valid to current subscribers of Harlequin Intrigue books.

Want to try two free books from another line?
Call 1-800-873-8635 or visit www.morefreebooks.com.

* Terms and prices subject to change without notice. N.Y. residents add applicable sales tax. Canadian residents will be charged applicable provincial taxes and GST. Offer not valid in Quebec. This offer is limited to one order per household. All orders subject to approval. Credit or debit balances in a customer's account(s) may be offset by any other outstanding balance owed by or to the customer. Please allow 4 to 6 weeks for delivery. Offer available while quantities last.

Your Privacy: Harlequin is committed to protecting your privacy. Our Privacy Policy is available online at www.eHarlequin.com or upon request from the Reader Service. From time to time we make our lists of customers available to reputable third parties who may have a product or service of interest to you. If you would prefer we not share your name and address, please check here.

HI08R

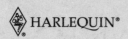 **HARLEQUIN®**

INTRIGUE®

COMING NEXT MONTH

#1077 THE SHERIFF'S SECRETARY by Carla Cassidy
Sheriff Lucas Jamison and secretary Mariah Harrington had always butted heads. But with her son's life in danger, Mariah trusts the sheriff to uncover a kidnapper hiding in their peaceful community—no matter the secrets revealed.

#1078 DANGEROUSLY ATTRACTIVE by Jenna Ryan
With a killer terrorizing police detective Vanessa Connor, Rick Maguire was assigned to protect her. But the enticing federal agent had to lead her further into danger if she was ever to be safe again.

#1079 A DOCTOR-NURSE ENCOUNTER by Carol Ericson
A relationship between Nurse Lacey Kirk and Dr. Nick Marino had always been expressly forbidden. But nothing could keep them apart amidst a string of deadly cover-ups and patients with secret identities.

#1080 UNDER SUSPICION, WITH CHILD by Elle James
The Curse of Raven's Cliff
Pregnant and alone, Jocelyne Baker believed her love life had been cursed. Yet only fate could have led her into the arms of Andrei Lagios. The cop wore away her defenses, even as the rest of the town grew wary of Jocelyne's return to town.

#1081 BENEATH THE BADGE by Rita Herron
The Silver Star of Texas: Cantara Hills Investigation
Nothing mattered more to Hayes Keller than the badge he wore. But while protecting heiress Taylor Landis, the heart of a real man in need of a good woman was soon exposed.

#1082 BODYGUARD FATHER by Alice Sharpe
Skye Brother Babies
Garrett Skye had a habit of taking on bad assignments, and now he was on the run. But he wasn't willing to leave his baby daughter behind, and that meant taking a stand with teacher Annie Ryder at his side.

www.eHarlequin.com